Zachariah Atwell Mudge

The Forest Boy

A Sketch of the Life of Abraham Lincoln for Young People

Zachariah Atwell Mudge

The Forest Boy
A Sketch of the Life of Abraham Lincoln for Young People

ISBN/EAN: 9783337415853

Printed in Europe, USA, Canada, Australia, Japan

Cover: Foto ©Andreas Hilbeck / pixelio.de

More available books at **www.hansebooks.com**

THE FOREST BOY:

A SKETCH OF THE

LIFE OF ABRAHAM LINCOLN.

For Young People.

By Z. A. MUDGE,

AUTHOR OF "LADY HUNTINGDON PORTRAYED," "THE CHRISTIAN STATESMAN,"
ETC., ETC.

FOUR ILLUSTRATIONS.

————◆◆————

NEW YORK:

PUBLISHED BY CARLTON & PORTER,

SUNDAY-SCHOOL UNION, 200 MULBERRY-STREET.

PREFACE.

WE have attempted in this volume a sketch of the life of ABRAHAM LINCOLN, adapted to young persons. None, so far as we know, of the biographies written since his death have had this special object in view.

We have given the facts in such detail that his general history may be understood, and have aimed so to group them together that his true picture may be seen from several points of observation. To do this we have made the chapters somewhat topical, but not to an extent to interrupt essentially the chronological order.

We have studied to bring out, for an example and inspiration to the young, that moral integrity and true goodness which were so prominent in Mr. Lincoln's character. We hope, therefore, that our book will be found worthy to be invited into the Sabbath-schools and Christian families of our country.

Much of the material here presented was found afloat in a fragmentary form, but derived, we are assured, from authentic sources.

We are indebted to the biography of Mr. Lincoln, by the Hon. J. H. BARRETT, for many facts of his early life; and to letters published in "The Independent," by Mr. CARPENTER, the artist, for sprightly illustrations of his later years.

We also acknowledge our indebtedness for many facts to the unrivaled Life of Lincoln by DR. HOLLAND.

Credit due to other sources is given in the course of the narrative.

We commend our unpretending volume to the attention of the young, from a deep conviction that the more they study the history of our late President, the more his character will interest and profit them.   Z. A. M.

QUINCY, Mass., *September*, 1866.

CONTENTS.

CHAPTER IX.

A STEP HIGHER.

CHAPTER X.

EARLY PUBLIC HONORS.

CHAPTER XI.

WINNING HIS WAY.

CHAPTER XII.

"RIDING THE CIRCUIT."

CHAPTER XVIII.

A TRIUMPH ACHIEVED.

CHAPTER XIX.

THE WHITE HOUSE IN PROSPECT.

CHAPTER XX.

THE VOICE OF THE PEOPLE.

CHAPTER XXI.

THE WHITE HOUSE ENTERED.

𝔍llustrations.

FOREST BOY.

———◆◆———

CHAPTER I.

THE PIONEERS.

THE beautiful valley of the Shenandoah, in Virginia, has recently been desolated by war. Here Sheridan gave Early the terrible blows which sent his army, broken and dismayed, back to their comrades behind their intrenchments of Richmond.

Almost one hundred years before this time, in 1780, there was living in this valley a family whose history the loyal people of the United States will always delight to study. It consisted of father, mother, three sons, and two daughters. The valley at this period was but thinly inhabited, there being only a few towns, and those far apart; while the Indian still pitched his wigwam on its sunny slopes, and the wild beasts roamed the forests. Yet this family caught the spirit of emigration. Daniel Boone, the famous hunter of those times, had taken a journey from his home in South Carolina to "The country of Kentucky," and returned with glowing accounts of its fertility and beauty. "The Western excitement" spread along the sea-shore to Virginia, and hundreds of families followed Boone in his new enterprise. The long journey, the great privations which it required, and even the dangers of the wilderness into which they went, afforded an excitement which they loved.

Such were the feelings of the family of whom we have just spoken. Its head was Abraham Lincoln, grandfather of the President. His youngest child, at this time about two years old, was Thomas, who became the father of Abraham, the DELIVERER of his country.

When this pioneer family broke up their home in the Shenandoah, and turned away

from the familiar scenes of their youth and the
graves of their fathers, they did not, it must be
remembered, step into the cars to be whirled,
in a few hours, to their chosen encampment.
A part of their journey lay through an almost
unbroken wilderness, where the feet of white
men had seldom ventured, and where the savage Indian still roamed. One rudely con-
structed wagon, or the backs of a few horses,
sufficed to carry the emigrants and their scanty
supply of goods. The trusty rifle, and perhaps
the berries by the wayside, supplied the crav-
ings of hunger; the pure stream gave them
drink, and the branches of the trees afforded
them shelter at mid-day and at night.

Mr. Lincoln did not end his weary journey
until he had passed nearly through Kentucky
to the valley of the Ohio River. He selected a
spot upon which nature had bestowed her richest gifts: the land was fertile, the game abundant, the scenery beautiful, and everything
seemed to say, God is here! Already the settlers from Virginia and the Carolinas began to

meet those who came down the Ohio from the North and East.

These lands were the hunting-grounds of the Indians; their fathers had followed the deer through these forests, and paddled their canoes upon these rivers, and the traces of their wigwams and their graves, for many generations, were here. It is not strange, therefore, that they claimed them, and looked with no friendly eyes upon the pale-faced strangers. They informed Daniel Boone in a very *savage* way that they did not bid him welcome: they made war upon all his company.

Just after Mr. Lincoln had erected his cabin, a large number of Indian warriors encamped not far from him. Daniel Boone assembled all the men of the scattered settlements of the country and gave them battle. Boone was defeated, many of his men killed, and his own son left wounded and dying in his arms. Inspired by a father's love, he plunged into the river near which the battle was fought, and swam with him to the opposite side, the Indians following close behind. When he reached the shore his boy was dead, and the father was obliged to leave his body in the hands of the savages to save his own life.

But the red man did not long appear in open fight. The whites increased in number, and were too skillful in their mode of warfare for the poor ignorant savages, who learned that their safer way was to hide in the bushes, or skulk behind trees, and pounce upon their foe as the tiger springs upon its unsuspecting prey. They came upon the settlers when they were not watching, killed the men, and often carried off the helpless women and children, after having burned their cabins.

About four years from the time Mr. Lincoln came to Kentucky, he was one day a short distance from his home chopping down trees. While he was thus busy, thinking, perhaps, of his children, and how he might better provide for their comfort, he did not know that the eyes of bloody savages, peering out from their hiding-places, were watching him. In a fatal

moment he set his loaded gun, which the pioneers ever kept near them, against a tree, and,
stepping a few rods away, lifted his ax to fell
a tree. At the instant the deadly arrow pierced
his body, and he dropped dead. His corpse
was found at the foot of the tree, the ax lying
beside it, and his gun where it was left.

It was a sad and gloomy day in the cabin of
these pioneers when they laid the head of the
family away in the grave, and thought that the
same bloody men who had killed him were
watching for their lives. But, though sorrowful, they were strong and brave; their women
had the courage of men, and the children the
stout hearts of older persons.

Soon after this Mrs. Lincoln took the children and went a little further east from the
Ohio, seeking, perhaps, the neighborhood of
friends, or thinking that the savages would not
attack her away from their favorite hunting
grounds.

Little Thomas was now only six years old.
The rough journey, the rude new home, and

the heavy bereavement, were a severe school for his tender age; and when only six more years had passed away he was obliged to leave his mother's cabin, and seek his living by labor among strangers. He grew up an ignorant, but not an idle and wicked man. He never learned to read, and he wrote only his own name, and that he had been taught to copy from the writing of another person, as boys copy pictures or trace maps; he did not even know the letters of which it was composed. But Thomas Lincoln had a strong hand and an honest heart. People loved the boy, and he found friends and work.

CHAPTER II.

LITTLE ABRAHAM.

THOMAS LINCOLN was twenty-eight years old when he married Nancy Hanks. This was in 1806. He had erected a log-cabin to receive his bride. It was such a house as his own hands could build in a few days with the aid of an ax only. It was situated by a little stream called Nolin Creek, in what is now Larue County, Kentucky. Heavy timber covered about two thirds of the land around them. This was the fertile land which the emigrants cleared for cultivation, the rest being open and barren, and either quite level, or swelling into mounds and hills. From the top of one of these hills, now called the "Blue Ball," the stream running by Mr. Lincoln's cabin door could be followed by the eye, in a fair day, as it curved around the hills and shot across the plains,

growing wider and deeper, until it emptied into
the Ohio River, twenty miles distant. In the
breezes, and from the trees, came a spirit of
freedom and peace to the happy couple. The
grandeur and beauty of nature about them
spoke of God in a voice both clear and elevat-
ing. Only *man* was vile, for as the savages
disappeared the white men came with their
slaves. But Thomas and Nancy Lincoln,
though poor, did not wish to become rich by
the unrewarded toil of others.

Mrs. Lincoln had come, in childhood, with
the emigrants from Virginia. She was from
her youth a member of the Baptist Church, but
her husband did not become a member until
after their marriage, and was won to Christ, it
may be, by her pious example.

Mr. Lincoln was a man of average height,
broad-chested, and well built. He was able
and willing to work, but ready to spend.
Good-natured himself, he did not suspect others
of ill will, even when he had good grounds of
distrust. He took the world too easy to

thrive, and was quite content to be what he was, a man of honest poverty.

Mrs. Lincoln was one of those remarkable women whom generations to come will delight to honor. She was of moderate height, slightly made, and of a sad, pale countenance. She was gentle and amiable, seeking the friendship and love of others. To her other gifts was added a mind of the first order. We shall see with what reason her son, long after her departure to be with Christ, called her his "angel mother." She was too frail a flower for exposure to the rude winds of pioneer life; a gem of great purity amid rough surroundings, where, indeed, such gems are often found. She could read, and she well improved the few books with which she was favored.

Thomas and Nancy had three children: Sarah, the first-born, Abraham, and Thomas. The latter died in infancy. Abraham was born, in the little log-cabin of which we have spoken, on the 12th of February, 1809. Such was the birthplace and such the parents of Abraham

Lincoln, whose name is now known throughout the world. Abraham was about two years old when his father moved from the log-cabin on Nolin Creek to one a little further east, three miles from what is now Hodgenville. It was not much expense or trouble to build a cabin, and so his father seems to have moved for apparently slight reasons, not having occasion to account the removal of the furniture a great item.

In this new home Abraham lived until he was seven years of age. It still stands, and has been frequently seen in the pictures as it now appears. This Lincoln cabin is plainly much decayed; but if we imagine the front to be tight, the fence perhaps away entirely, we shall see the humble home of Abraham Lincoln nearly the same as when he lived in it.

We cannot think that Abraham and his sister Sarah were able to carry on their childhood's sports within doors; but their playground was ample. The tall trees of the surrounding forests which overshadowed the soil prevented the growth of underbrush or tangled vines. Nature's carpet of green and brown was spread for their feet. There were no neighbors with sensitive ears to chide their hearty shout or merry laugh. Abraham could dam the little streams, and form mimic waterfalls; while Sarah on the hillside was making evergreen wreaths for her own hat, or leafy crowns for her brother's brow. If they chose the more invigorating amusement of "hide and seek," what grand hiding-places were the tree trunks, and what a run they might have without danger of bolting against a table or pitching over a chair!

Though the children could not *play* in-doors, they could, and did, when not able or not inclined to go out, do something better. At this time they were not old enough to help their mother in the household labor. It is said that there were two ways in which their parents delighted to interest and instruct them at the fireside. The first and most important was the reading by the mother, who had a pleasant way of making remarks, and of exciting talk concerning that which was read. The father told

them stories of the early settlers of Virginia
and Kentucky, and the incidents, often repeated
in his mother's cabin, of the long journey to
the West. He had his tale, too, of Indian
cruelties, which aroused the ardent spirit of
Abraham. Sarah was better suited with the
accounts of autumn feasts among neighbors,
and of their winter merry-making. Mr. Lincoln told a story well, and he was fully re-
warded when he saw the happy countenances
of Sarah and Abraham, as they sat on their
little stools at his feet, listening with sparkling
eyes. Mrs. Lincoln's amusement of the children was accompanied by a more valuable
instruction, and even her husband greatly prof-
ited by her pleasant words. At this time there
were only two books, so far as we can learn, in
the Lincoln cabin, the Bible and Catechism.
From these precious truths were taught. The
word of God became more valuable to Abraham than the highest honors or the greatest
treasures. Sitting at his mother's feet, he listened to those Bible stories which have such

wonderful power to interest and instruct, and
of which the good never tire. Even at this
early age he had a keen, inquiring mind, and
asked many questions concerning Joseph, Mo-
ses, Samuel, David, and other famous men,
which his mother took great pleasure in answering. When he was alone with Sarah he
had his wise opinions to offer concerning what
his mother had read. These sayings, though
childish, were little sparks from the same glowing mind which so amused and instructed
others in later years.

CHAPTER III.

A NEW HOME.

IN 1816, when Abraham was in his eighth year, his father began to think of a new home. He seemed to like moving; and the excitement attending a new situation, different scenes, and untried difficulties, was the stimulus to activity in which he delighted. Things were uninteresting to pioneers after they became familiar; at least this appears to have been the case with Mr. Lincoln. We do not think his thoughtful, frail wife felt just so, yet she possessed a heroic as well as loving spirit, and where her dear ones went she followed with a calm trust in the God of providence.

Mr. Lincoln could readily find some excuse for his desire to push on further West. The titles to lands in Kentucky were much disputed at this time. Old settlers were sometimes obliged to give up their homes and improved lands to new claimants, because the records of the courts had not been carefully kept. Daniel Boone, whose right to whatever land in Kentucky he could reasonably desire must have been as good as any claim could be, except that of the Indians, was dispossessed of nearly all his estate by later comers. Mr. Lincoln hoped that further west his home would be more secure.

He thought, too, of the evils of slavery, which were spreading over this new country, and did not wish his children to grow up under its influence. Yet his son never thought that this was a principal reason for his removal. He could not then see the sinfulness of slavery as good men have since seen it; but he saw enough to convince him that he and his family would be happier and more prosperous in a free state.

While Mr. Lincoln was planning in reference to his new home, and talking the matter over with his wife, a man by the name of Colby came into his cabin. He wanted to buy the farm, and does not appear to have been afraid

that Mr. Lincoln's title was not good. They
soon made a bargain, Colby agreeing to pay for
the house and cultivated lands, for the whole
real estate of Thomas Lincoln, three hundred
dollars! The very convenient "greenback"
currency, which passes alike at the counter in
New York or Boston and the cabin of the West,
was not of course in circulation then, and gold
and silver were seldom seen among the buyers
and sellers of those forest homes. We should
not, however, have "guessed" that the purchaser of the farm paid for it mostly in *whisky;*
but such was the case. ' He agreed to give ten
barrels of that article, valued at two hundred
and eighty dollars, and twenty dollars in cash.

It must be remembered that these were days
when even good men thought that the daily
use of intoxicating liquors as a drink might be
good; but they have learned better now, and
the light that has been given to the people of
the country through the temperance cause ren-
ders the making, selling, or using the poisonous
article as a drink, a sin. Mr. Lincoln learned

in after years that the wise treatment of whisky was neither to touch, taste, nor handle it.

Mr. Lincoln was to have a short time in which to make his preparations to move. He at once built a flatboat, and launched it upon a stream a short distance from his cabin, called the Rolling Fork. Into this flatboat (a boat much like *gondolas* of the Eastern shores) he put his ten barrels of whisky and the heavy articles of the farm and cabin. He then started off to find a spot for his new home, leaving his family until his return. He floated down the Rolling Fork into the Ohio River, and then along the shore safely for some distance. But the most careful navigator is sometimes wrecked; so Mr. Lincoln, though doubtless very carefully watching to avoid every danger, as a man would naturally do whose boat bore his entire wealth, was upset, and his cargo plunged into the rushing waters. He must have been near some landing-place, as he obtained immediate aid in righting his boat and saving a few barrels of whisky and some other valuable articles. His loss, however, must have been very severe, and he doubtless continued his voyage with a sorrowful heart. Landing at Thompson's Ferry, Indiana, he gave a man his flatboat to carry him and his goods into the interior. Their team dragged slowly along a poor road ; sometimes they were obliged to stop and open one through the woods with the ax. They arrived at last, after journeying eighteen miles, at a location whose fertility and beauty invited them to stop.

Leaving his goods in the care of a neighbor, about two miles off, Mr. Lincoln returned with the wagon to Thompson's Ferry, and having crossed the Ohio, walked home.

The days of Mr. Lincoln's absence were busy and thoughtful ones with Mrs. Lincoln and the children. It was hard parting with a spot where all the sights and sounds reminded them of happy days which were past. They visited the grave of little baby Thomas, and shed over it their parting tears. This last incident deeply affected Abraham, and he often referred to it in the years of his manhood with much emotion.

Everything being ready, the bedding and the few remaining household articles were packed upon three horses, and the family, riding, but frequently on foot, began their journey. In seven days they reached the spot selected by Mr. Lincoln. Here a log-cabin was built by the assistance of a neighbor, and they were soon surrounded with such comforts as belong to these humble homes. This house contained only one room below, and a small attic made by laying rough boards overhead; this was reached by a ladder, and was Abraham's bedroom. His bed was a bearskin thrown upon the boards, with a blanket for covering. The family of course lived in the room below, which served also as the sleeping room of Sarah and the parents. Skins put up at the doors shut out the piercing winds, but when the cold was severe all slept near the glowing fire. The bedstead of Mr. and Mrs. Lincoln was made by a rough framework of nails and slabs fitted against the side of the cabin, with a sack of dried leaves thrown upon it. A table was con-

structed of a wide slab, with legs inserted into
the rounded side, and three stools were made in
the same way of smaller pieces.

Their "mill" was, in form, like the "mortar
and pestle" of a New England Thanksgiving
day; "the mortar" being about three feet of
the trunk of a large tree, whose end had been
burnt out to hold the corn, and the "pestle"
being a heavy piece of wood hung on "a sweep,"
as buckets are sometimes hung on "well sweeps."
This contrivance of the pioneers saved a long
and difficult journey to the regular mill. During the winter, which was now near, Mr. Lincoln was engaged in chopping down trees and
clearing the land for the spring planting. The
comfort of the family was much aided by the
sale of the whisky which was saved from the
wreck upon the Ohio. The trusty gun, that
true friend of the pioneer, brought them plenty
of game. The fire burned cheerfully within
the cabin of Thomas and Nancy Lincoln, and
we will enter to see what besides they had to
make them happy.

3

CHAPTER IV.

SCHOOLS AND BOOKS.

Not long before Abraham left Kentucky, and when he was about seven years of age, Zechariah Riney opened a school for the children of the neighborhood of Nolin Creek. Of the school-house in which the scholars daily assembled we know nothing; but we may safely imagine that some log-cabin, or a room of the plainest frame building, was gladly accepted for the purpose. Riney taught three months, and Abraham attended, commencing to read and write. Caleb Hazel soon took the school, and taught another three months. During these six months Abraham made rapid improvement, and at the close of the last term was able to read in the family the plain portions of the Bible, greatly to the gratification of his parents. Soon after the removal to Indiana there were

others who taught for a little while at a time;
and Abraham's parents, though so very poor,
always succeeded in making some arrangement
by which he could have the benefit of these
opportunities. These teachers were men of
little education; but they could read, and
write, and "cipher," and these were attainments which rendered them very useful to the
pioneer children. Indeed, but few of the
parents could see the utility of studying books
beyond this, and some regarded even this small
degree of learning as quite unnecessary.

Abraham's entire school privileges extended
through one year only. But at the end of this
time he could write a tolerably correct and
intelligible letter. It was not only by the
teaching which he received in school that he
was enabled to do this; he diligently practiced
at home. Though pens, paper, and ink were
scarce in his father's cabin, charcoal and birch
bark were not, and these answered in their
stead. Sitting down by the cheerful fire, he
wrote, over and over again, the copy set him

by his teacher. Sarah was astonished at his success, and felt proud of her ambitious brother. The father and mother looked approvingly at their boy, and silently prayed that God would make him a good and useful man.

The only text-book which Abraham possessed during these school-days was an old copy of Dillworth's speller. This and the Bible and Catechism were constantly in his hands during his leisure hours, when he was not practicing with his birch-bark copy-books. No doubt he delighted "to spell" his sister Sarah, and to puzzle even older persons with the hard words he had learned. Boys of his age who love their studies are apt to go humming round the house, showing off their learning to the other members of the family.

Having now a good start in reading, other books fell into his hand from time to time. The kind providence of God finds food for such hungry little minds, just as he provides food and clothing for their bodies. "Esop's Fables" was the next book of which he became the

owner. Its pictures, though coarse in compari-
son with those of our present juvenile works,
were exceedingly attractive, and its lessons,
taught by the stories of beasts and birds, deeply
impressed him. His pleasure in sitting by the
blazing fire during the winter evenings was
greatly increased as he read its pages, and
repeated its fables to Sarah. It seemed to the
eight-year-old boy a long step up the ladder
of knowledge. No out-door sport, however
much he delighted in it, could keep him a long
time from his books.

On one occasion his love for a gun was
greatly excited. His father had gone with his
ax to work in the forest. Abraham looked
through the openings between the logs of the
cabin, and saw, not far off, a flock of wild
turkeys. He had never fired a gun, but at
once determined to try. Taking his father's
fowling-piece from its place, he pointed it
through the crevice of the logs and fired, kill-
ing one of the finest of the flock. This was
considered a wonderful shot for such a boy,

and Abraham was flattered more for it than for his ambition to get useful knowledge. Yet he never learned to love the life of a hunter. Gunning seemed an idle way of spending time, except when it was necessary to obtain food.

Just in good time, when Esop's Fables had been well read, and its lessons deeply impressed upon his mind, "Bunyan's Pilgrim's Progress" was obtained. He was prepared for just such kind of truth as it imparted, being led to think of lessons more important than those of the Fables; not new, indeed, but set forth in a new and impressive manner. He followed the Pilgrim through his many conflicts to the gates of the Celestial City, and felt that he understood better what he had been taught from the Bible and his mother's lips. It afforded his mother new topics for religious conversation, in which she breathed into his tender mind her living Christian spirit.

The next book with which Abraham was enriched was "Weems's Life of Washington." This was the most exciting, though not the

best book he had read.   It was full of the dash-
ing adventures of the southern heroes of the
Revolution.   Its stories of battles were told
with great spirit, and its life-pictures of George
Washington were deeply impressive.   A burning love for his country, which was never
extinguished, was kindled by its pages.   He
remarked many years afterward, " I remember
all the accounts there given of the battle-fields
and struggles for the liberties of the country."
When he laid down this book to get wood for
his mother's fire, or to aid his father in the
work of the farm, he was *thinking* about
Washington and the men who fought with him.
It was always one of his peculiarities, that he
thought a great deal of what he read.   He had
many questions to ask his parents about it,
many, indeed, which they could not answer.
He says of himself, in looking back upon these
days: "I recollect thinking then, boy even
though I was, that there must have been something more than common that these men
struggled for."

The next book read was the Life of Henry
Clay. Mr. Clay was then "the young man
eloquent," whose fame was filling the land.
Many thought that no place of honor in the
nation was so high as not to be within reach of
his brilliant talents. God designed Abraham
Lincoln for a politician and statesman, and this
book came into his hands to lay early in his
mind the foundation of a deep interest in the
great questions which concerned his country's
good.

Abraham was now about nine years of age.
His appearance spoke of his humble condition.
His pants and coat were made of dressed buck-
skin, such as was worn by the Indians, and his
cap was of raccoon skin. He was happy in
his Indiana home, and in the glowing ambition which his books had inspired within his
youthful heart. But the tender sensibilities of
his mind were to be made strong by the blasts
of adversity, and the disciplining of severe
bereavement.

CHAPTER V.

THE GREAT BEREAVEMENT.

THERE was a gloom pervading the cabin of
Thomas Lincoln, when, less than two years after
he came to Indiana, his wife began to sink
under the inroads of consumption. The faithful wife and loving mother was about to leave
her forest home for a mansion in heaven. Her
spirit toward her family became more than ever
tender. She spoke to them of her hope in the
Saviour, and of the peace which passes all understanding, conferred by the merits of his blood.
Abraham and Sarah listened with affectionate
interest. Already she seemed to them " an angel mother," and kindly they anticipated all her
wants; and when she became too weak to leave
her bed, they moved gently about the cabin,
fearing to make any noise which might disquiet
her sensitive nature. Abraham read to her in

a subdued voice the exceeding great and precious promises which she had loved so well in
health.   It was thus that God's word made impressions upon his mind too sacred ever to be
effaced.   It was his mother's dying support, and
it spoke peace to his own troubled mind in the
hours of great sorrow.   When at last his mother's lifeless form lay before him, his Bible
seemed his best friend, as indeed it was.

There were but few friends to call at the
Lincoln home in this time of bereavement, yet
these few cordially tendered their aid and sympathy.

Mrs. Lincoln was buried in a simple manner,
under the shadow of the forest trees.   Abraham
lingered upon the grave and wept.   There was
no minister of the Gospel near, but the influence of the preaching of earlier years held a
silent sway over his heart.

The Lincoln family had never been favored
with regular public religious service.   When
they were in Kentucky they received the occasional visits to their neighborhood of the faith-

ful itinerants. They preached in the open forests, or in the friendly cabin, to which the
people gathered for many miles around. Their
words strengthened the faith of the few believ-
ers among the settlers, and aroused the slumber-
ing feelings of the careless. They had been
much-loved seasons to the now sainted mother,
and Abraham remembered them for her sake,
and felt anew their power. There was one
among these itinerants whom he called to mind
with special love. His name was Elkins, a
Baptist preacher. A few months after Mrs.
Lincoln's death, the broken circle of the cabin,
sitting about the fireside, talked of Parson Elkins, and the mother's grave unhonored by any
religious service. It was decided that Abraham
should write, inviting him to come and preach
her funeral sermon. It was Abraham's first
letter, and in a holy service written. With deep
interest the family waited a reply. In due
season it came, the good man willingly prom-
ising to come at an appointed time. Faithful
to his promise, he made the difficult journey of

nearly one hundred miles to perform the labor
of love. Abraham had diligently extended the
notice to the settlers in every direction for
twenty miles. Parson·Elkins entered the Lincoln cabin, and there learned how well his
Christian friend had died; he had observed in
earlier days how well she had *lived*. At the
appointed time he went forth to meet the people around her grave. It was a beautiful Sabbath morning. Notice had spread beyond the
limits of Abraham's most distant rides to carry
it, and at an early hour the congregation began
to assemble. Those who have not seen such
gatherings cannot understand the depth of interest which is manifested in the pains taken to
reach the place. In ox-teams, on the backs of
mules and horses, in carriages of rude construction, and on foot; over difficult roads and
through paths scarcely discernible, they press
to the sacred spot. The old come bending
upon the tops of their staves, the strong laborers from their toil, and children in their mothers' arms. No member of these scattered com-

Young Lincoln at his Mother's Grave.

munities is uninterested in these solemn gatherings.

The minister took his stand at the head of
the grave. Before him, sitting upon the ground,
or in vehicles drawn up on the outskirts of the
multitude, or standing leaning against the trees,
was a congregation as solemn and as eager for
the bread of life as could be found in more cultivated society. The hymn was read, and sung
in one of the simple melodies so common among
the congregations of these early itinerants;
simple, but full of deep emotional power. The
prayer, and the sermon that followed, were not
listened to with a mere cold respect for serious
things. The audience were eager to hear, and
not a word was lost. The preacher spoke of
Christ as the "resurrection and the life," and
closed with a eulogy on the character of the departed saint. Her *life* had fully prepared her
friends and neighbors to receive the glowing
words of praise.

As the people slowly dispersed, Abraham
stood silent and alone at the grave. His great

loss came home to his heart with fresh power, and he inwardly resolved to follow his mother's example in loving God and his word.

Abraham and Sarah became dearer to each other after their mother's death. Upon the latter, now about eleven years of age, devolved, for a year at least, the in-door care of the family. But her brother, whose fondness for reading and study kept him at home, was ever ready to help. Kindness to others, and a willingness to bear a portion of their burdens, was always a trait in Abraham Lincoln's character, and clearly showed itself now toward his sister. He read to her the family Bible, and studied it alone, until he could repeat a large portion of it; when in after years he was in great trouble, its sweet promises came to him with much comfort.

Abraham's father married about a year after his mother's death. This second wife was a kind guardian of Abraham and his sister, and they soon learned to love her and her children, older than himself, whom she brought into the

family. His weight of grief abated in a few
years. He had not learned to love his mother's
memory less, but God kindly provides a balm at
the hands of time for human woe, since we cannot worthily serve him if we always weep.

At the end of four years from his mother's
death · Sarah died, at the age of fifteen., This
renewed cause of grief to her sensitive and loving brother was seen for a long time in his sad
countenance. Indeed, these early sorrows were
never forgotten; perhaps the burden of other
years kept them in remembrance. The painter
of "The Signing of the Emancipation Proclamation" says that Abraham Lincoln's countenance was the saddest he ever saw.

CHAPTER VI.

EARLY MANLINESS.

As Abraham grew to early manhood he became
tall and strong beyond his years.   He rendered
good service to the family with his ax in felling
trees and clearing the land, and with the hoe in
planting and cultivating.   But he did not vaunt
himself on account of his physical powers, and,
though stronger than most of his associates, and
frequently, in a playful manner, wrestling and .
running with them, he never used his superiority to annoy them.   He was more ambitious to
excel in knowledge, and to use that knowledge
for the good of others.   He became the general
letter-writer of his neighborhood.   The pioneers, being away from their early friends in the
older states, and many of them not knowing
how to write, used his hand and pen with great
pleasure.   It is evident that they regarded him as

no ordinary young man, and even then learned to look up to him as their leader; and he constantly strove to be worthy of this high esteem.

Not long after the death of his mother a Mr. Crawford opened a school in his neighborhood. He is one of the teachers of whom we have spoken, under whom Abraham obtained the beginning of his knowledge of arithmetic. Mr. Crawford was a very kind-hearted man, and, seeing Abraham's love for books, lent him Ramsay's Life of Washington. This was a great prize. Weems had excited his imagination by highly colored incidents of the life and times of the Father of his country; Ramsay gave him more solid information. He carried his prize home as a miner would have done a piece of quartz heavy with shining gold. He bounded into the cabin, holding up his treasure to his father and Sarah, (for this was before her death,) his face flushed with excitement. They were both pleased with his good fortune, and Mr. Lincoln promised himself a great treat in hearing it read.

4

After the toils of the day the sadness of the
broken family circle was for the time relieved
while Abraham sat, with his back to the fire,
holding up the borrowed volume to its light, by
which he read aloud. Candles and lamps were
luxuries not freely used by the pioneers. The
father sat on one side of the fireplace, resting
his chin upon his hand and his elbow upon the
table, looking his son in the face with parental
pride. He was thinking quite as much of the
reader as of the great and good man of whom
he was reading. Sarah sat upon the other side,
her fingers busily employed while she listened,
and her eyes now and then resting with delight.
upon her noble brother. This was a humble
literary circle, it may be, but its waves of influence were to be extended, by the blessing of
God, to the ends of the earth and to the latest
generations!

Abraham's interest in this book became absorbing. He was generally prompt to obey any
requirement of his father, and did not have the
bad habit of waiting for a second request. He

was also ready to answer promptly and kindly
any call from his sister for assistance; but he
was now so deeply interested in his book that
he lingered when called to his daily task. This
was not right, and he soon saw his error and
corrected it.

A sad accident to this volume grew out of
this intense interest. Being called suddenly to
leave it, he laid it down in his hurry upon the
open window seat; he should have taken a moment more of time and put it in a safe place.
While he was absent a shower came up, and the
book was badly wet. With manly honesty, but
with a heavy heart, Abraham took the book to
Mr. Crawford, explained to him how it happened, and offered to pay for the damage in
work. Mr. Crawford proposed to *sell* him the
book instead of taking pay for the injury. To
this Abraham readily agreed, and " pulled fod-
der" three days for it. When at length he
returned home he felt that his labor had made
him rich.

The following incident shows how much

kindness to others was united with his manly bearing. One evening, when returning, with several young men, from a neighbor's, where they had been raising the frame of a new house, he discovered a horse, saddled and bridled, feeding by the roadside. He immediately recognized it as the horse of an acquaintance, who was frequently drunk. The young men at once searched for the owner, and found him chilled and helpless upon the ground. Abraham's companions sneeringly remarked that they would not trouble themselves further about the miserable fellow, and that he might lie there until he was sober enough to go home. But Abraham Lincoln could never turn away from any person, however undeserving, to whom he might be of real benefit. He begged his companions to lift the man upon his shoulders. He then carried him to the nearest house. After he had sent to his father an account of what had happened, he remained and nursed the poor inebriate until he became able to take care of himself. Abraham then returned home

with the pleasant thought that he had probably
saved the man's life.

Every manly effort gives increased desire for
other efforts, and more strength in their performance, and such was Abraham's experience.
When he was about eighteen years of age, the
harvest of the Lincoln farm proved more than
was needed for home consumption ; the surplus
had been raised by his own hands, so he formed
the resolution of building a small flatboat and
taking this produce to New Orleans. To this
Mrs. Lincoln objected. Though not her own son,
she loved Abraham. The distance was great,
and the enterprise was full of dangers. Besides,
she would miss him so much from the log-cabin
home ! But he greatly desired to go, though he
declared he would not stir a step without her
consent; he wanted to see more of the world,
and to be doing more for the family. The matter was talked over by the father and mother,
till they finally decided that he might go. If
he was successful, the money obtained would
enable them to purchase many things which

they very much needed. They knew his manly spirit and good judgment, and felt great confidence that he would succeed.

Abraham immediately commenced building his flatboat. He had a few tools, and was fond of showing his skill in using them. His boat was soon about done. One day, while he stood looking at it, thinking how he could make it stronger, more convenient, or improve it in any way, a steamer stopped opposite the landing. There were no wharves at that time on the Ohio, so the steamers paused for the passengers to go ashore or to be sent aboard in boats. While the steamer was waiting, two gentlemen came to the landing in a carriage, bringing heavy trunks. They looked at several boats which were ready for their accommodation, and finally stopped and looked at Abraham's. Approaching him, they said, " Whose boat is this, young man ? "

" It is mine," he replied with an honest pride.

" Will you carry us and our trunks to the steamer ? " they inquired again.

"Certainly," said Abraham, seizing the trunks and placing them in his boat. He hoped to earn fifty or seventy-five cents, besides accommodating the strangers. The gentlemen sat upon the trunks while Abraham sculled them to the steamer. They stepped on board, and he lifted their trunks to the deck. The steamer was about to start, when he called to the strangers, reminding them that they had not paid him. Thus prompted, they each threw into his boat a silver half dollar. He was delighted. It was the first dollar he had ever earned. He could scarcely believe that he, a poor boy, had, by his own hard labor, earned a dollar in less than a day. When Mr. Lincoln, in after years, told this story, he added: "This may seem like a very little thing, and it seems to me now like a trifle. But it was a most important incident in my life. The world seemed wider and fairer before me. I was a more hopeful and confident being from that time."

We know nothing more of Abraham's first trip down the Mississippi, but are con-

fident its results met the expectations of his
friends.

Returning to his father's farm, he cheerfully
resumed his former toil.   At one time he took
a grist of corn upon the back of the family
horse, and rode fifty miles to get it ground.
The mill was a very poor one, turned by horse
power.   The customers had to wait their turn,
and then use their own horse to move the mill-
stones.   Abraham's turn had come, and having
attached his horse to a long pole by which the
mill was put in motion, he was following her
with a switch and "a cluck."   The horse, perhaps resenting the double work of bearing the
corn to mill through so great a distance, and
grinding it when there, suddenly lifted her heels
and kicked her master, stunning him by the
blow.   The moment he came to himself he finished his "cluck," and, jumping up, compelled
the horse to complete the job and bear him and
his meal home.

The monotony of his daily duties was broken
soon after by a new employment.   The nearest

point on the Ohio to his father's farm was Troy, a small town at the mouth of Anderson's Creek. Here for a few months he acted as ferryman, thus adding to his knowledge of river life.

A year after Abraham's first voyage down the Mississippi in his own small flatboat, a trading neighbor proposed a much more important trip. He desired him to take a flatboat cargo to the sugar plantations near New Orleans. The trader proposed to invest a considerable amount of money in the enterprise, so that to him as well as to Abraham it was an important affair. But he knew Abraham's honesty and good management. He believed that he would make the trip profitable.

Abraham set out on the long voyage of eighteen hundred miles with the son of his employer. They sailed only about as fast as the current of the "Father of Waters" carried them. With a long oar extending from each side, and one at the stern, to keep the boat in the deep water, and prevent it from striking the "snags" and "sawyers," they moved quietly along. Some-

times the river spread itself over a great extent
of country, and they were at a loss to keep the
channel. At other times it rushed through a
narrow " cut off," and compelled them to work
with great vigor and skill to prevent their boat
from being upset or dashed against the shore.

They had a little cabin on board, in which
they cooked, and into which they crawled for
rest and shelter. When the darkness or the
weather prevented them from sailing safely,
they tied the boat up to the shore.

Arriving at last among the plantations between Natchez and New Orleans, they began
to think of a landing and a sale. One night
they fastened their boat to the banks of the
river, and lay down to sleep. When the night
was well advanced, Abraham, who was not easily taken by surprise, even during the sleeping
hours, heard the sound of stealthy steps approaching the boat. He shouted, " Who's there?"
There was no answer, but the sudden dash of
seven negroes toward the boat, bent on plunder,
and perhaps murder. They had awoke no

puny, cowardly opponent. Abraham seized a
club, and with giant blows knocked the first
three comers into the river. The others, seeing
Abraham's companion springing to the rescue,
and intimidated by the rough handling given
to their comrades, turned to escape. But their
retreat was as unsuccessful as their attack.
They were overtaken and severely punished.
The others scrambled from the river, and having
no further relish for the fight, ran away. The
victors, thinking the negroes might return with
fresh recruits in large numbers, cast off their
lines, and, drifting down the river a mile or
two, drew up again to the shore and waited for
the morning. They were exhausted and a little
wounded by the conflict, but not seriously hurt.

Having sold their cargo to good advantage,
they disposed of their flatboat and returned
home.

Abraham's pay for his services was at the
rate of ten dollars a month. This was small
return indeed, but he received large compensa-
tion in the increased confidence of his friends,

and in the future development of a manly character.

He was now nearly a man in years, and much larger than ordinary men. He was six feet and four inches in height. No bad habits had weakened his body or clouded his mind. He used no intoxicating drinks, and turned with manly contempt from tobacco. He was not guilty of the low sin of swearing, and his word was never doubted by those who knew him. Though his education from books had advanced no further than the capability of reading, writing, and " ciphering," he had a brave heart and good conscience. Thus prepared, he was about to begin life anew.

CHAPTER VII.

BEGINNING ANEW.

THE family of Thomas Lincoln had been in Indiana about fourteen years. Great changes had taken place, but there were many ties to bind them to their home. Here were the graves of their loved ones. Many acres of land had been brought into cultivation by severe toil. Later emigrants had settled about them, and rendered themselves dear by acts of friendship. But the location was thought to be unhealthy. The heavy growth of trees rendered the labor of any further clearing of the land very great. Exciting accounts had come from Illinois of the fertile prairie lands, skirted by woods, and well watered by streams. Dennis Hanks, a relative of Mr. Lincoln's first wife, was sent to "spy out" this land and bring them word again. He returned, and reported that it needed only the plow to prepare it for the seed, and that abundant crops could be secured with little labor.

Thus stimulated to indulge his moving propensity, Abraham's father sold at once his Indiana farm, and in March, 1830, was on his way to Illinois. His wife's daughters and their husbands were of the company. They traveled with ox-teams, into which their goods were loaded. The family rode or walked, as the way permitted. The spring rains had swollen the rivers, and given to the rich soil that condition which made it difficult at times for the teams to move. One of them was driven by Abraham. He had just completed his twenty-first year, and was a man in strength and energy. While crossing the bottom lands of the Kaskaskia River, the men of the family waded through water several feet deep. Persons of less energy would have given up in despair, or been diverted from their purpose. But Abraham, leading the rest with his team, overcame the obstacles by the same persistency which, in after years,

made him triumphant in nobler enterprises. In
fifteen days the party traveled two hundred
miles, and reached Macon County, Illinois. A
spot was selected, ten miles west of Decatur,
on the north side of the Sangamon River, on
prairie land bordered by a fine growth of trees.

The first business was to provide a new home.
Abraham assisted his father in building a cabin,
and his relative, John Hanks, came and lent a
helping hand to the work. The house was cut
and split from the forest trees, and was completed in four days. It was nine logs, or about
eighteen feet, high. The material for the doors,
floor, and shingling, were split from the logs.
It was eighteen feet long and sixteen wide. It
had neither window sashes nor glass, but a hole
in the shutters, over which a piece of oiled paper
was drawn, gave them a little light when the
cold required the shutters to be closed. Only a
few nails were used about the building, and
these were brought from Indiana. It was a
genuine *union* cabin, nine different kinds of
wood entering into its material. The tools used

about it were a common ax, broad ax, hand-saw, and "a drawer knife." A few out-buildings were erected near it, and the home was completed!

This cabin was exhibited during the summer of 1865, on Boston Common, by the Mr. Hanks who helped build it. It has since been removed by Mr. Barnum to his museum in New York.

The house being done, Abraham aided in splitting rails enough to inclose a ten acre lot. A good friend of his has said that "he split rails well." He did well all common work, and thus prepared himself for higher and more difficult labor.

Having inclosed, he assisted in plowing and planting the ten acre field. Thus having seen his father's family comfortably started in their new position, Abraham spent the rest of the farming season with neighboring planters, receiving monthly wages. During this time he broke up fifty acres of prairie land, using four yoke of oxen. This toil afforded him only a living. But his mind was much occupied with

nobler purposes. He read such useful books as
came within his reach, and pursued his studies
in the branches of knowledge already commenced.

He was working at one time during the summer on the farm of a Mr. Taylor, and boarding
in the family of Mr. Brown. At this period
there were in that section of country no public
houses, and travelers were accommodated at the
private residences. One evening a man rode
up to Mr. Brown's fence, and inquired if he
could stay over night. Mr. Brown replied that
he could give him something to eat, and take
care of his horse, but he could not lodge him
unless he consented to sleep with the hired man.
The stranger hesitated about accepting this condition, and asked where the hired man was.
"You can come and see," replied Mr. Brown.
So the stranger dismounted, and Mr. Brown led
him round where Abraham was lying in the
shadow of the house, at full length upon the
ground, deeply interested in the book he was
reading. "There he is," said Mr. Brown,

5

pointing to Abraham. The stranger scanned him from head to foot as he arose, his sunburnt face glowing with good-nature and intelligence. " He will do," said the stranger ; and, as Abraham concluded, upon a survey of the visitor, that *he* would do, they slept together that night.

The family of Abraham's father were disappointed in their new location. They had sought for a more healthy region than that of Indiana. But here they were all attacked, in the first autumn, with the fever and ague. This was a new difficulty for the pioneers, and a very serious one. It was of no avail that the soil was fertile and the scenery beautiful. It was not enough that their neighbors were kind and their cabin comfortable. Without health, all was marred. So in the spring Abraham assisted in moving the family to Coles County. Here his father lived until he had completed his seventy-third year. He ever received from his son the most devoted and affectionate attention. He died July 17, 1852.

CHAPTER VIII.

ENERGY AND HONESTY.

ABRAHAM did not fully leave the parental home until his father's removal to Coles County. He then became only a visitor there, having his residence where he could find the means of living, and of increasing his stock of book knowledge. One who knew him well at this period, having split rails with him, says he was an ungainly, rough-looking young man. His trowsers were made of coarse material, cut tight at the ankles, and were worn through on both knees. Though he was known to be very poor, yet such was the esteem in which his character was held, and the pleasure felt in his social qualities, that he was a welcome guest in every family. He spared no pains to obtain work, walking sometimes several miles before and after his day's toil; yet his cheerful spirit never received the prompting which comes from a full purse.

Wishing at one time to obtain a pair of new pants for those "out at the knees," it became a study to know how he should pay for them. He finally made a bargain with Mrs. Nancy Miller for the necessary yards of jean, dyed with white walnut bark, agreeing to split four hundred rails for each yard of cloth.

One so willing to work as Mr. Lincoln could not long be without a paying employment. During his first winter in Illinois a Mr. Offutt, a trader, proposed to engage him to take, in the spring, a flatboat to New Orleans. Abraham's experience in this hazardous business, and his great energy, made him just the man for the service, and this kind of business suited his enterprising spirit. When the spring opened he purchased a canoe, and, taking John Hanks and John D. Johnston as his companions in the voyage, proceeded down the Sangamon River to Springfield. They here met Offutt, but he had failed to purchase a flatboat according to the previous arrangement. The three voyagers immediately went about seven miles northwest of Springfield, to Sangamon town, on the river of the same name, and built and launched a flatboat. They did the work at the rate of twelve dollars a month, chopping out logs for the material from heavy timber, and sawing them into planks with " a whip-saw." They floated their boat down the river below New Salem, and landed at a point where a drove of hogs were to be taken on board. The hogs were wild, having grown up in the woods, and would be neither coaxed nor driven into the boat. ' The business of taking in freight was for a brief time at a standstill; but Mr. Lincoln was not to be turned aside from his purpose by the stubbornness of a drove of hogs. Seizing them, one by one, he dragged them along, in spite of their noisy protests and vigorous resistance, and tumbled them into the boat. Then, after completing their cargo with a variety of articles of less troublesome freight, they started for New Orleans. Mr. Hanks, fearing a longer

absence from his family than he had supposed,
left them at St. Louis, and returned home.
The trip was made by the other two, the boat
and cargo sold at good advantage, and the settlement made with Mr. Offutt to his satisfaction.   In fact he was so well pleased with Mr.
Lincoln, that he offered him further employment.   Mr. Offutt had a store and mill at New
Salem.   These, during his trading excursions
about the country, he had intrusted to clerks,
who had disgusted and driven away his customers by their bad manners, and cheated him in
their accounts.   He gave the charge of this mill
and store to Mr. Lincoln, who brought to the
new position industry and fidelity.   He knew
what ought to be done, and did it promptly.
The people of the whole region soon learned to
like the new clerk, and flocked to the store both
to buy goods and to hear his pleasant talk.
The business increased, and so did the gains of
his employer, for they did not now stop in the
clerk's pocket, or slip through the clerk's fingers for his own gratification.   His exact hon-

esty became well known, but his way of showing it was sometimes a little amusing. A
woman came into the store and bought goods
to the amount of two dollars and six cents.
She paid that sum, and left the store. When
she had gone, Mr. Lincoln cast up the figures
again to assure himself that he was right, and,
in doing so, ascertained that he had taken just
six cents too much. It was toward the close of
the business hours, so, shutting the store, he
walked between two and three miles, found the
customer, paid the balance due, and returned
with the satisfaction of having acted squarely
up to a high sense of right.

At another time, just as he was about to
close the store for the night, a woman called
for half a pound of tea. It was weighed, as he
supposed, and the customer, having paid the
price, departed. On opening the store in the
morning he observed a four-ounce weight in
the scales. It was at once plain to Mr. Lincoln that he had given the woman but half as
much tea as she paid for. He immediately

locked the store, and, without first getting his breakfast, took a long walk to deliver the full weight.

Since "a good name is rather to be chosen than great riches," Abraham Lincoln had now acquired a priceless treasure. His honesty became as widely known as his tall figure, attractive stories, and great physical power. "Honest" became from this time the prefix to his name; his rough companions always spoke of him as "Honest Abe;" and the loyal masses of his whole country delighted, a few years after, with more hearty good-will than good taste, to ring the changes upon the name of "Honest Abe," varying it by the still more distasteful appellation of "Old Abe." Our youthful readers will prefer to know and speak of him as the pure principled man, honest Abraham Lincoln.

At one time, while Mr. Lincoln was waiting upon several ladies, a boastful ruffian came into the store, using toward him the most abusive language, and challenging him to fight. Mr.

Lincoln begged of him not to use such language, especially as ladies were present. To this gentleness the braggart replied by shaking his fists, and shouting, "Let the man come on who dares to tell me what I shall say." Mr. Lincoln replied that if he would wait until the ladies were gone he would try to satisfy him, and this he succeeded in doing, though not in the way his annoyer sought. The two stepping out of the store, he easily laid the boaster upon his back, and, holding him in his giant grasp with one hand, and reaching out the other for a handful of "smart weed," he rubbed it freely upon his face and into his eyes, until he cried out like a whipped spaniel. Mr. Lincoln then, with the utmost good-nature, which had not been for a moment disturbed during the whole incident, brought water and tenderly aided in alleviating the pain of the just punishment he had inflicted. The rowdy, thoroughly humbled by his defeat, and completely won by the kind manner in which it was done, became the steady and warm friend of his victor.

Another incident, somewhat like the one just
given, illustrates still more the character of the
pioneer community in which Mr. Lincoln lived,
as well as his own peculiarities.

There was about New Salem a company
called the "Clary's Grove Boys," composed of
the strongest, fleetest, bravest, and most unprin-
cipled young men of the vicinity. They assumed the authority of "regulators;" that is,
they banded together to whip those who refused
to acknowledge their rule. They were especially severe toward strangers coming to reside
among them. They required such to race,
wrestle, or fight with one of their number. Of
course Mr. Lincoln was considered an excellent
subject for such demands; and, as he had always
been used to trying his physical strength with
his associates, he was not displeased with the
proposed trial. The Clary's Boys selected as
their champion a young man by the name of
Armstrong, who was charged with the duty of
wrestling with Mr. Lincoln, and laying him on
his back. The whole gang gathered around to

see the sport. It was soon apparent, to the vexation of "The Boys," that Armstrong had met with more than his match; but with a meanness belonging to such low minds, they proceeded to indulge in "foul play," striking and tripping Mr. Lincoln, until he was thrown down. The Clary's Boys shouted in triumph, and Lincoln, instead of getting angry at their unfairness, and thus affording them a pretext to unite and flog him, laughed as heartily as any of them. They could neither match his strong arm nor overcome his good temper. Their envy and desire to annoy him were turned into admiration, and they gave him an urgent invitation to become one of their number. But he preferred more profitable employment and better company. He had made them his friends, and their good-will soon after helped him in advancing *a step higher.*

CHAPTER IX.

A STEP HIGHER.

HAVING become known as a strong and brave man, and having secured the confidence of all in his honesty, Mr. Lincoln determined to earn a higher reputation for intelligence. While in Offutt's store, after having read all the books within his reach, he resolved to make himself acquainted with English grammar. But he could not obtain a grammar for some time after he had made this resolution. He at last heard of a man, eight miles from New Salem, who owned one. He at once walked to his house and borrowed it. It was Kirkham's, a work which had an extensive popularity in the West and South thirty-five years ago. It was an admirable text-book for one endeavoring to learn without a teacher. It contained simple statements and examples for beginners under each rule ; in critical notes at the bottom of the page it gave the necessary information for more advanced study. Mr. Lincoln took his prize, and stole away as often as possible to make himself master of its contents. In the mean time Mr. Offutt, who was a general trader, having his business spread widely over the country, failed, and the store and mill were shut up. Mr. Lincoln was now without any regular employment, but was not idle. There was a hill just out of the village to which he often resorted with his grammar. When he came to a point which he did not understand, he made a note of it and applied to his friend, Mr. L. M. Green, for explanation.

Thus persevering, he mastered the book. After having done this, he playfully remarked to a friend, that if that was what he called science, he thought he could "subdue another."

Mr. Lincoln began now to be conscious of his great powers, and the eminence to which he might attain. He remarked to his friend Green, during a familiar conversation, that none of his family had become known to fame, but he felt that he might perhaps excel them in this respect. He had talked with some great men, and did not perceive that they differed very much from other men.

He became at this time connected with the debating clubs of New Salem and vicinity, and often walked six or seven miles to attend their meetings. One of these clubs met in an old store at New Salem. It was here that he made his first speech. He called the discussions "practicing polemics." Like such debates generally among young men, these "polemics" were very amusing. They, however, gave Mr. Lincoln confidence in his own powers of argument and utterance.

The following incident, related to us by his friend and relative, John Hanks, must have occurred at this time, and shows that he improved his first opportunity to try his gifts before a public audience. He went one day to Decatur, about ten miles from New Salem, with an ox-team. He was barefooted, wore a jacket and pants of the coarsest material, and had on his head a wide-rimmed straw hat, not in the best state of repair. The soil of the muddy road covered his feet and ankles.

There was at this time much excitement throughout Illinois concerning questions then before the legislature at Vandalia, and a political meeting was being held at Decatur in reference to them. A gray-headed man had just commenced to address, out doors, a crowd of people as Mr. Lincoln arrived. He listened attentively to the speaker, and when he closed John Hanks whispered, "Abe, you can beat that." Mr. Lincoln shook his head, but continued to watch the proceedings of the meeting. The next speaker was a genteelly dressed and fluent young man. To his speech also Mr. Lincoln gave the closest attention, and when he sat down Hanks touched Lincoln again, saying, "Abe, I *know* you can beat that."

"O no, John, I guess not," replied Mr. Lincoln modestly.

But Hanks was determined to call his friend

out, and he commenced canvassing for him among the crowd. He soon rallied a party who began to call for " Abe Lincoln." It was perhaps the first utterance of the public voice, local and faint then, which afterward became so loud and universal that it elevated him to the most responsible position in the world.

A salt box was procured, and, mounting it, " all accoutered as he was," he began his speech.* The crowd gathered about him; but at first his appearance repelled attention, and the noise drowned his voice. But soon his intelligent face, good sense, and his clear, full utterance secured for him a favorable hearing, which continued to the close of a long speech. The question upon which he spoke was in reference to an appropriation by the legislature to remove the obstructions to navigation in the Sangamon River. Perhaps it had been before the debating club at New Salem; at any rate he was master of the subject, and when he stepped down from the salt box he was greeted with

* See Frontispiece.

hearty cheers. The gray-headed man who had first spoken was excited to envy by the superior popularity with the people of the uncouth stranger. Approaching him in an excited manner, he exclaimed, " Young man, where did you learn so much?"

"In my father's log-cabin," answered Mr. Lincoln promptly.

Stimulated by this success, his ambition for reading, study, and close thought took a new start. A gentleman called upon him one day, and found him lying upon a trundle-bed on his back, covered with books and papers, intensely absorbed in study, but rocking a cradle with his foot, thus contriving to improve his mind, and at the same time help his landlady by caring for her babe.

Mr. Lincoln had now become known not only for his bravery, strength, and intelligence, but for his sound judgment in practical matters. He was frequently requested to decide disputed claims, to settle quarrels, to answer knotty questions, and to give his opinion concerning business of grave importance. He was welcome in every social circle, in spite of his poverty and uncultivated manners. His position was indeed one in advance of his previous attainments.

CHAPTER X.

EARLY PUBLIC HONORS.

WHILE Mr. Lincoln was out of employment a small cloud of war gathered in the West. Black Hawk, chief of the Sacs Indians, collected a company of warriors from his own and neighboring tribes, and came east toward the old hunting-grounds of his fathers. Being threatened by a United States force greater than his own, he cunningly sued for peace, and promised to keep the old treaty, which bound his tribe to remain on the west of the Mississippi River. But this was only a pretext for gaining time to gather more warriors, and make greater preparations for the fight. The next spring he returned in great force. Being warned back by the general in command of the government troops, he sent an answer of defiance. This aroused the white people of the

state, and the governor called for volunteers.
Mr. Lincoln was among the first of his vicinity
to enlist, and, when a company was made up,
he was surprised by an invitation from many of
his comrades to stand as a candidate in the
election of its captain.   There was but one
other candidate, a man of influence in the
county, who had at one time employed Mr.
Lincoln, and treated him in an arbitrary and
oppressive manner.   The election was conducted in a peculiar way.   The candidates took
their places a little distance apart, and the
members of the company walked up to and
stood with the one they preferred.   One after
another marched to the side of Mr. Lincoln,
until a large majority had thus voted for him.
Most of the minority then left his opponent,
making his election nearly unanimous.   His
old employer and opposer was keenly mortified,
while Mr. Lincoln felt a glow of honest pride
at his success.   It was his first public honor,
and from this time the world looked brighter,
and the pathway full of encouragement.   He

frequently referred to it in subsequent years, and declared that no election of a later period so much gratified him. He had been largely indebted for this honor to his old opponents whom he had vanquished in boxing, wrestling, and running.

Black Hawk was too shrewd to fight a decisive battle with his enemies, but broke his forces up into small bands, and ravaged the country. This compelled the volunteers to make long and forced marches without bringing the Indians to a fight, or seeing any immediate results of their toil and sacrifices. When, therefore, their thirty days of enlistment had expired, the most of them, declaring that they had seen enough of such warfare, accepted their discharge, and returned home. Mr. Lincoln, however, enlisted as a private for another thirty days, and at its expiration re-enlisted, and remained until the war closed. Black Hawk was pursued by a portion of the United States troops, and finally captured, with most of his fighting men. Mr. Lincoln was not in the fight, but returned home with a good name, the officers respecting him for his intelligence and fidelity to his responsibilities, and the soldiers loving him for his care of them as their commander, and for his story-telling, wrestling habits as a companion.

In referring to this military experience in a political speech many years after, Mr. Lincoln playfully remarked, that though he was not on the battle-field during the fighting, he saw the place soon after; and though he did not break his sword, not having any to break, he did bend his musket pretty badly at one time. He declared that, though he did not charge upon the Indians, not having seen any, he made charges upon the wild onions, and had many bloody struggles with the mosquitoes; and, though never faint from the loss of blood, he was often truly very hungry.

He had not been at home ten days before the election for the state legislature took place. Through the prompting of his late comrades in arms, he was put up as a candidate. This was an unexpected honor, and affected him greatly by its expression of good-will. As the ticket on which his name was placed was that of the party greatly in the minority in the county, he was not elected, but obtained nearly the entire vote of all parties in his immediate neighborhood where he was best known.

Being now about twenty-eight years of age, he began to feel keenly the necessity of a more permanent employment, and seriously purposed to learn the blacksmith's trade ; but before he had taken any steps to carry out this intention, an opportunity occurred of entering into business with another person, with whom he united in buying out a stock of goods of a small retail store in New Salem. His friend, Mr. W. G. Greene, became security for the payment of the goods, which were purchased on credit. The partner proving worthless both in business and character, the enterprise entirely failed of success, and Mr. Greene was obliged to pay a large part of the indebtedness of the concern. The debt thus contracted to Greene, which Mr. Lin-

coln humorously called "the national debt," he
paid many years afterward to the uttermost
penny, though his partner was equally responsible, and though the creditor had moved into
Tennessee, and had well-nigh forgotten it.

Mr. Lincoln being again out of business,
since, as he remarked, his store was "winked
out," he gladly accepted from President Jackson an appointment as postmaster of a small
office at New Salem. The income did not pay
for constant attention to the office, so when he
went out on other business he took the mail in
the top of his hat. Persons inquiring for letters or papers hunted up the postmaster, who
answered their inquiries after taking off his hat
and turning over its contents. The greatest
benefit he derived from this appointment was
the privilege of reading all the papers taken
in the vicinity, which were probably few in
number.

But the office was the occasion of a beautiful
illustration of his honesty. It being either discontinued or removed to a distant place, he

squared up his accounts for a settlement with the government. Many years afterward, while sitting in a law office, a gentleman called and inquired for Abraham Lincoln. "I am the man," said Mr. Lincoln, stepping forward. The gentleman then presented the government's bill against him. For a moment he looked perplexed. His friends, who were sitting by, observing this, offered to lend him the required sum. He made no reply, but his countenance suddenly lighted up with a happy thought. He went to his bookcase and took down a little trunk containing a small package of coin wrapped in a cotton rag. "How much is your demand?" he inquired of the stranger. "Seventeen dollars," was the reply. The package was put into his hands containing just that amount. When the agent of the Post-Office department had left, Mr. Lincoln quietly remarked that he never used money which did not belong to him. During much of the time in which this money had been thus laid by he had been very poor, and the temporary use of it would have been a great relief; but he had never indulged the thought of touching it.

Again looking round for business, an unexpected opening was presented. John Calhoun, then surveyor of Sangamon County, being much pressed with business, offered to employ Mr. Lincoln. The latter knew nothing of surveying, but he resolved to learn. Borrowing some books of Mr. Calhoun, he bent his strong will and clear intellect to the work. He was soon ready to begin, and received from his employer the business near New Salem. He procured a compass and a chain, (or, as some say, a grape-vine instead of a chain,) and commenced his new employment.

This was a progressive step in his career. He continued in the business more than twelve months, sparing no pains to render his services profitable to his employers and creditable to himself, and he had the satisfaction of knowing, many years afterward, that though he had laid out one whole township, the accuracy of his work was never questioned.

His engagements as a surveyor received one unpleasant interruption. His compass and chain were taken and sold for a debt growing out of the unfortunate partnership concern. But they fell into the hands of a friend, who quietly restored them to him.

CHAPTER XI.

WINNING HIS WAY.

MR. LINCOLN steadily increased in the favor of
the people.   Those who saw him most frequently were most deeply impressed with his
goodness of heart and greatness of mind.   His
old friend, Offutt, who had observed him closely
in his store, exclaimed in enthusiastic admiration, "Lincoln knows more than any man in
the United States."

The governor of Indiana, after a conversation with him, was astonished at his understanding and the extent of his information, and
declared that the young man had talents enough
for a president of the United States.

His friend Greene was so impressed with his
greatness, that, when he was spending a college
vacation at New Salem, he took the occasion to
introduce him to some college friends, among

whom was Mr. Richard Yates, afterward governor of Illinois. They found Lincoln lying
upon his back on a cellar-door, reading a news-
paper, his hands, as usual, hard with the toils of
labor, and his face blackened by exposure to
the sun and wind. The college boys were
doubtless amused that their friend Greene should
esteem such a man one of the New Salem
" lions ;" but a short interview led them fully to
accord with his high estimation. Mr. Lincoln
entertained the visitors by quotations from a
volume of Burns's poems, the whole of which
seemed stored in his memory, and surprised them
by his familiarity with Shakspeare and keen
perception of his beauties. Greene invited
Lincoln to dine with him in company with the
college boys. Feeling awkward at the table in
consequence of the presence of those to whom
his modesty attributed great superiority, he upset his bowl of bread and milk ; but his friend,
Mrs. Greene, playfully diverted the attention of
the company, and relieved his embarrassment.

A trait of Mr. Lincoln's character, which became very marked in subsequent life, began especially to attract notice at this time. This was his readiness to devise means to overcome great and unexpected obstacles in the way of the accomplishment of anything which he had undertaken.

He was one day in the Sangamon River trying to float a flatboat over a milldam. With his pantaloons rolled up above his knees, he jumped into the shallow water, and, putting his shoulder to the stern of the boat, pushed its prow over the dam. Here it struck fast, being partially filled with water, and consequently too heavy for even his great strength. Bailing it out was the most apparent way of relieving the difficulty, but this would take much time and labor. Mr. Lincoln seized an auger, which was at hand, and bored a hole in that part of the bottom which projected over the dam, thus letting the water run out; then, plugging up the hole, he easily pushed the boat into the river below the falls, and continued his voyage.

Mr. Lincoln was one day in Springfield

attending a book auction, when his attention was arrested by a copy of Blackstone. He immediately bought it, and carried it home with much the same feelings which he had in his boyhood on finding a copy of the Life of Washington. His friends had, in a complimentary manner, often said, " Lincoln, you would make a capital lawyer." He doubtless felt that God had given him a power of occupying a public position ; and, thus moved, he read this volume with absorbing interest. But a new opening for promotion soon occurred. Two years had passed away since his failure of an election to the state legislature. In 1834 he was again nominated to represent Sangamon County. The custom in the West requiring candidates to lecture among the people on questions of public interest, he bought a horse to enable him to visit the several towns and villages of his district for this purpose, selling his compass and chain to procure the necessary funds. When the canvass was over he sold his horse and purchased his instruments again. This time his nomination was a success, resulting in his election by an unusually large majority.

During these electioneering tours Mr. Lincoln renewed his acquaintance with Mr. John T. Stuart, a lawyer of large practice in Springfield, who had been with him in the Black Hawk war. Mr. Stuart was confirmed in his previous conviction that Mr. Lincoln was a remarkable young man, and he advised him to study law, offering to lend him books for this purpose. By this encouragement his earlier resolutions in the same direction were strengthened, and he walked to Springfield, a distance of twenty-two miles, obtained "a back-load" of books, and returned the same day to New Salem.

He now alternated between surveying and studying, doing just enough of the former to keep himself economically fed and clothed. His favorite place of study was under an oak on a hillside, where he had "subdued" Kirkham's grammar. Here, lying on the ground, only changing his position to keep in the shade, he became so absorbed in the great principles of. the law that he was in a measure lost to the common affairs of life. In fact, those persons who did not understand his character called him partially insane. He cared little for this, and still less for the ordinary social enjoyments of life, of which he now mostly denied himself, as he mastered, one after another, the foundation truths of his chosen profession.

When the time came for the commencement of the legislature, Mr. Lincoln took his personal effects upon his shoulders and walked to Vandalia, the capital of the state, a distance of one hundred miles.

He was the youngest member of the House, with one exception, and, of course, entirely unacquainted with the forms of law-making. He therefore wisely made no speeches, but observed closely the details of the daily business. A friend of this period says that his modesty was seen and acknowledged by all. This attractive quality lessened the unfavorable impression made upon strangers by his person and manner. His dress was "Kentucky jean," made in the style of the times, and, however unpretending, was a great improvement over his apparel of any former occasion.

When the session was over he walked back to New Salem and resumed his studies and surveying.

In 1836 he was again a candidate for the legislature, and during the canvass became more prominently before the people. He wrote for the political papers statements of his sentiments, and held public discussions with his opponents. One of these is remembered for the successful manner with which he conducted it, securing victory from seeming defeat. Mr. Lincoln was associated on the occasion with an able friend, who was to take an equal share on his side of the discussion. This friend had spoken, and been fiercely assailed in reply by a keen opponent. The friend, chafing under the attack, desired to repel it immediately. But it was Mr. Lincoln's turn, and he, feeling the full inspiration of the occasion, could not give way. He ascended the platform, and commenced in a slow, argumentative manner. His friends at first appeared anxious, and his opponents retained briefly the air of triumph inspired by the last speaker; but Mr. Lincoln gradually showed the weakness of his antagonist's positions by strong arguments, plainly and forcibly presented, and won the favorable convictions of the audience. Having exposed his false reasoning, he heaped contempt upon it by wit and ridicule, his tall figure becoming erect as he proceeded, while his countenance lost its habitually sad expression, and his eye its mildness, as the fire of eloquence flashed from every feature of his face. The audience interrupted him by frequent and loud applause. His triumph was complete, and his reputation was greatly increased as one of the ablest debaters of the state.

On his return to the legislature he took a more active part than during its previous term. The antislavery question was just beginning seriously to divide the two great political parties. Neither of them was willing to own the hated name of abolitionist, and both sought the favor of the slaveholders.

A set of resolutions strongly in this spirit passed the legislature, with only two opposing votes, those of Abraham Lincoln and Dan Stone, both of Sangamon County. They entered upon the journal of the House their protest against them, written, it is understood, by the former. It was his first antislavery record, and a good one. It stated moderately his views on the peculiar institution, and the questions connected with it. They were, as far as they went, such as he avowed when elected President, and as he maintained through life. It required moral courage to publish them at this time and in this manner, for they were unpopular even among his own political friends.

When the session was over he walked home, in company with the other representatives from Sangamon County. The whole delegation, nine in number, were remarkably tall, none of them being less than six feet. The

wits called them " the long nine." The company traveled on horseback, except Mr. Lincoln, who kept up with them on foot. His
dress was thin, and he complained on the way
of being cold. One of his companions, looking
roguishly at his large feet, drily replied, " Of
course you must be cold, there's so much of you
on the ground." Mr. Lincoln enjoyed the joke,
and laughed as heartily as any of them. He
was ever ready, with pleasant story or humorous remark, to relieve the weariness of the way.

Mr. Lincoln was again out of business, but he
stood in a position in advance of any he had
before occupied. He had obtained a fair
knowledge of the common branches of an English education; he had read several works on
scientific subjects, giving special attention to
geology; he had become known through the
state as a popular debater, and an able politician; and he was fairly initiated into the
forms of practical legislation. He was therefore prepared for the wider sphere upon which
he was about to enter.

CHAPTER XII.

"RIDING THE CIRCUIT."

MR. LINCOLN became a lawyer in 1836, and the following spring was invited by his old friend, Major Stuart, of Springfield, to enter his office as a partner. This was an unexpected and pleasant compliment. He was without experience, and without extensive reading in the law, and only twenty-eight years of age. Major Stuart was favorably known as a lawyer, and was established in a large practice.

Mr. Lincoln removed to Springfield, and became a member of the family of a gentleman of high social standing. The people of Springfield remembered their indebtedness to his influence in the removal of the state capital to their city, and expressed their gratitude by electing him to the legislature of 1838–40. He was again elected in 1840, and, at the end of the legislative term, declined further honors of this kind.

During his eight years of membership of the legislature he rose constantly in influence, commanding the entire vote of his party for the speakership. He was, in fact, recognized as their leader in the House. His speeches were strong in argument, clear in statement, striking, and often beautiful in illustration. His pleasantry and keen wit fixed the attention of the most indifferent. When occasion required, he could silence an opponent by sarcasm and ridicule. The following is an illustration: A certain member of the House constantly indulged in quibbling objections to proposed measures. He saw a violation of the Constitution of the state where others saw only conformity to its requirements. Mr. Lincoln's friends said to him, " Lincoln, you can silence that man, and you ought to do it." " I'll try," he replied, his countenance lighting with a humorous expression. Quite soon there was an opportunity. Mr. Lincoln had proposed a bill

which the watchful member denounced as un-
constitutional.   Mr. Lincoln arose to reply,
and, with a laughable kind of gravity, said that
the gentleman reminded him of a man in his
neighborhood, whom he described in such a
manner that all eyes were turned toward his
opponent as the person intended.   "Now this
man," he continued, "while dressing one morning, looked out of the window and saw a squirrel, as he thought, on the limb of a tree near
the house.   Seizing his rifle, he fired at it, but,
to his astonishment, the saucy animal was
neither hit nor frightened.   He fired again and
again, but there the squirrel remained with
provoking coolness.   The man, looking at his
gun and then at the tree, exclaimed to his
son, who stood at his side, ' Boy, what's the
matter with my gun that I can't shoot that
squirrel ? '

"' Don't see any squirrel,' replied the boy.

"' Don't see any squirrel! there he sits half
up that tree ! '

"' No, father,' replied the son, looking into

his father's face, 'there aint any squirrel; it's a louse on your eyebrow that you see.'"

The members enjoyed a hearty laugh at the offender's expense, and he troubled them no more.

When not in the legislature, Mr. Lincoln was pursuing his studies and practice, and soon became known as a successful pleader. He delighted to advocate the case of those whom he knew to be wronged, but would not defend the cause of the guilty. If he discovered, in the course of the trial, that he was on the wrong side, he lost all interest, and ceased to make any exertion.

Once, while engaged with an associate in a prosecution, he became satisfied that their client's cause was not a good one, and he refused to make the plea. His associate, less scrupulous, persisted, and obtained a decision in their favor. The fee was nine hundred dollars, half of which was tendered to Mr. Lincoln, but he refused to accept a single cent of it.

His honesty was strongly illustrated by the

way he kept his accounts with his law partner.
When he had taken a fee in his absence, he put
one half of it into his own pocket, and folded
up the other half, putting it away carefully by
itself, labeled "Billy," the name by which he
familiarly addressed him.   One day his partner
asked him why he did not make a record of the
amount and for the time use the whole.   "Because," replied Mr. Lincoln, "I promised my
mother never to use money belonging to another
person."

He had another singular habit as a lawyer.
Having studied both sides of the case he was
managing, when he stood up in court to defend
it, he presented with perfect fairness all that
could be said against as well as for his position.
When, therefore, his opponent rose to speak,
he found, to his great embarrassment, his arguments already anticipated and answered.

This fairness, together with his good-nature
and aptness at story telling, made him a favorite
among all the men of his profession.   It was
the practice of the lawyers to follow the judge

through the district he traveled to attend the
courts, they going on horseback or in "gigs."
This they called "riding the circuit." They
put up together at the country taverns, and expected a merry time when Mr. Lincoln appeared
among them. We cannot say that on such
occasions he always told such stories as the
good and pure could fully approve. Abraham
Lincoln learned, as all in similar circumstances
will learn, that "evil communications corrupt
good manners;" and he was quick to follow
the better way when favored with the example
of those of higher culture and stricter morals.

In the early part of his career as a lawyer
he was engaged in a case which caused much
amusement, and showed his aptness in putting
the truth in the most striking light. There
were two men of one neighborhood each of
whom owned a mare and its colt. The colts
resembled each other in a very remarkable
manner, and, having both strayed away, it was
natural that, on the return of one only, each
owner should claim it as his animal. Thirty-

four men testified on the side of one claimant, and thirty were equally confident in giving their testimony for the other. All the witnesses were good and true men, and all had known the colts well. Thus puzzled, they very sensibly agreed to leave the decision to the mothers of the colts. On an appointed day the mares were brought to a public place, and a large company assembled to witness the decision. The colt was brought forward with the mare it had met in a pasture when it returned, and with which it had since been living on familiar terms, not having during this time seen the other one; the other mare was then introduced to the inclosure, and instantly the colt sprang to her side, with earnest demonstrations of joy. No efforts could cause it to express a different choice, or to hesitate in its preference. Nature had spoken, and all were satisfied except the selfish claimant on the other side; he appealed to the law.

Mr. Lincoln, in arguing the case for the defendant, made the following ingenious statement: " Here, gentlemen," he said, " is a case concerning which a large number of honest men differ. Thirty-four men are against my client, while on his side are thirty men and the conduct of the colt. You may not feel *sure* which is right, but you must decide in favor of that side which you think is most likely to be right. Now, gentlemen, on which side would you be willing to bet? on which most readily risk a picayune? The side on which you would risk a picayune is the side in favor of which you must give your decision."

The jury were plain men, and this was an easy test which aided them in deciding the case, and they gave it at once to Mr. Lincoln's client.

CHAPTER XIII.

THE RESCUE.

WHILE Mr. Lincoln was studying law he found an occasional home in the cabin of a man whose name was Armstrong, the same person whom the Clary's Grove boys had chosen to lay him upon his back in a wrestling match when he first came to New Salem. It will be recollected that Armstrong had found more than his equal in fair play; but he begged Lincoln to call it "a drawn game," and was ever after his fast friend.

Many years had passed away, and Armstrong had died, leaving his widow and children dependent mainly upon his eldest son. An incident in connection with this son gave occasion for Mr. Lincoln to show his characteristic ability and goodness. The story is thus told by one witnessing most of the circumstances: "A

young man had been killed in a riotous and
confused fight in the night time at a camp-
meeting, and one of his associates stated that
the death wound was inflicted by young Armstrong.   A preliminary examination was gone
into, at which the accuser testified so positively,
that there seemed no doubt of the guilt of the
prisoner, and therefore he was held for trial.
As is too often the case, the bloody act caused
an undue degree of excitement in the public
mind.   Every improper incident in the life of
the prisoner, each act which bore the least
semblance to rowdyism, each schoolboy quarrel,
was suddenly remembered and magnified, until
they pictured him as a fiend of the most horrible hue.   As these rumors spread abroad they
were received as gospel truth, and a feverish
desire for vengeance seized upon the infatuated
populace, while only prison bars prevented a
horrible death at the hands of a mob.

"The events were heralded in the county
papers, painted in the highest colors, accompanied by rejoicings over the certainty of

punishment being meted out to the guilty party.

"The prisoner, overwhelmed by the circumstances under which he found himself placed, fell into a melancholy condition bordering on despair, and the widowed mother, looking through her tears, saw no cause for hope from earthly aid.

"At this juncture the widow received a letter from Mr. Lincoln, volunteering his service in an effort to save the youth from the impending stroke. Gladly was his aid accepted, although it seemed impossible for even his sagacity to prevail in such a desperate case; but the heart of the attorney was in his work, and he set about it with a will that knew no such word as fail. Feeling that the poisoned condition of the public mind was such as to preclude the possibility of impanneling an impartial jury in the court having jurisdiction, he procured a change of place and a postponement of the trial. He then went studiously to work, unraveling the history of the case, and satisfied

himself that his client was a victim of malice,
and that the statements of the accuser were a
tissue of falsehoods.

"When the trial was called on, the prisoner,
pale and emaciated, with hopelessness written
on every feature, and accompanied by his half-
hoping, half-despairing mother, whose only hope
was in a mother's belief of her son's innocence,
in the justice of the God she worshiped, and
in the noble counsel, who, without hope of fee
or reward upon earth, had undertaken the
cause, took his seat in the prisoner's box, and
with a stony firmness, listened to the reading
of the indictment.   Lincoln sat quietly by,
while the large auditory looked on him as
though wondering what he could say in defense of one whose guilt they regarded as
certain.

"The examination of witnesses for the state
was begun, and a well-arranged mass of evidence, circumstantial and positive, was introduced, which seemed to inclose the prisoner
beyond the possibility of escape.   The counsel

8

for the defense propounded but few questions,
and those of a character which excited no un-
easiness on the part of the opposing lawyer,
merely, in most cases, requiring the main witnesses to be definite as to the time and place.
When the evidence against the prisoner was
ended, Lincoln introduced a few witnesses to
remove some wrong impressions in regard to
the previous character of Armstrong, who,
though somewhat rowdyish, had never been
known to commit a vicious act; to show also
that a greater degree of ill feeling existed between the prisoner and his accuser, than between the prisoner and the person who was
killed.

"The prosecutor felt that the case was a clear
one, and his opening speech was brief and formal.   Lincoln arose, while a deathly silence
pervaded the vast audience, and, in a clear and
moderate tone, began his argument.   Slowly
and carefully he reviewed the testimony, pointing out the hitherto unobserved discrepancies
in the statements of the principal witness.

That which seemed plain and plausible he made appear as crooked as a serpent's path. The witness had said that the affair took place at a certain hour in the evening, and that by the aid of a brightly shining moon, he saw the prisoner inflict the death-blow by a slung-shot. Mr. Lincoln showed that at the hour referred to the moon had not yet appeared above the horizon, and consequently the whole tale was a fabrication.

"An almost instantaneous change seemed to have been wrought in the minds of his auditors, and the verdict of 'not guilty' was at the end of every tongue. But the advocate was not content with this intellectual achievement. His whole being had for months been bound up in this work of gratitude and mercy; and as the lava of the overcharged crater bursts from its imprisonment, so great thoughts and burning words leaped forth from the soul of the eloquent Lincoln. He drew a picture of the perjurer so horrid and ghastly that the accuser could sit under it no longer, but reeled and staggered from the court-room, while the audience fancied they could see the brand upon his brow. Then, in words of thrilling pathos, Lincoln appealed to the jurors, as the fathers of sons who might become fatherless, and husbands of wives who might be widowed, to yield to no previous impressions, no ill-founded prejudice, but to do the prisoner justice; and as he alluded to the debt of gratitude he owed to the boy's father, tears were seen to fall from many eyes.

"It was near night when he concluded by saying that if justice was done, as he believed it would be, before the sun should set it would shine upon the prisoner a free man. The jury retired, and the court adjourned for the day. Half an hour had not elapsed when, as the officers of the court and the volunteer attorney sat at the table of their hotel, a messenger announced that the jury had returned to their seats. All repaired immediately to the court-house, and while the prisoner was coming from the jail, the court-room was filled to overflow-

ing with citizens from the town. When the
prisoner and his mother entered, silence reigned
as completely as if the house had been empty.
The foreman of the jury, in answer to the usual
inquiry from the court, delivered the verdict of
'not guilty.' The widow dropped into the
arms of her son, who lifted her up, and told
her to look upon him as before, free and inno-
cent. Then with the words, 'Where is Mr.
Lincoln?' he rushed across the room and
grasped the hand of his deliverer, while his
heart was too full for utterance. Lincoln
turned his eyes toward the west, where the
sun was still lingering in view, and then turning to the youth, said, 'It is not yet sundown,
and you are free.'"

CHAPTER XIV.

FURTHER INCIDENTS OF "THE CIRCUIT."

THE story of "the rescue" is only one among many evidences of Abraham Lincoln's kindness of heart during his career as a lawyer. Even the sufferings of a brute excited his pity.

He was once riding his circuit in a "a gig" alone, and while crossing a stream skirted with deep mud he saw a pig almost buried in the mire. The poor thing was nearly exhausted, and its feeble struggles pleaded touchingly for assistance. Mr. Lincoln looked at the pig, and then at the new suit of clothes which he had just begun to wear. He certainly could not help the pig without spoiling the clothes; besides, he said to himself, *it's only a pig!* Thus endeavoring to satisfy his sense of right, he rode on. But the suffering brute was still before him, causing a most unpleasant burden of

mind. When he had rode two miles, so dissat-
isfied did he feel that he turned back to the
stream. Tying his horse to a tree, taking off
his coat, boots, and stockings, and rolling up his
pants, he gathered rails from a fence in the vicinity, and built a foot-road to the pig. He
then laid hold of him and dragged him from
his perilous situation, much to the disparage-
ment of his new pants. The pig no doubt
grunted his thanks; but his deliverer was un-
generous enough to himself as he rode on,
pondering, as he remarked afterward, upon
"the philosophy of the incident," to refer his
benevolent act to the low desire of getting rid
of his own burden of mind!

When Mr. Lincoln had become established in
his law practice, and had attained considerable
popularity, he did not forget his humble relations, and the poor among his acquaintance of
earlier years. He often walked many miles, and
neglected more distinguished company, to visit
such friends.

As he was going out one evening, after a

hard day's work in court, to call upon an old
lady, his companions tried to persuade him to
remain with them, urging that the distance was
great, that he was weary, and that they desired
his company.   "O, I *must* go," he replied res-
olutely, "aunty's heart would break if I left
town without calling upon her."

Those who were unfortunate in person or
purse always excited Mr. Lincoln's sympathy.
A Mr. Cogdal became embarrassed in business,
and having employed him to settle up his
affairs, gave him, at the close, a note for the
amount of his fee.   Not long after Mr. Cogdal
was blown up by the accidental discharge of
some gunpowder, and lost the use of his arm.
Thus poor and crippled, he met Mr. Lincoln
one day, who inquired kindly after his welfare.
Cogdal replied, "I am getting along poor
enough, and I have been thinking about that
note."   Mr. Lincoln interrupted him by taking
the note from his pocket and saying, as he put
it into his hand, "There, think no more about
it."   Cogdal was about to decline the gener-

ous offer, but Mr. Lincoln walked abruptly away.

A widow of a revolutionary soldier came into Mr. Lincoln's law office in great trouble. She had employed a pension agent to obtain her claim against the government, and he had charged her two hundred dollars for his services. When, on careful inquiry, he found that there could be no doubt about her statement, he was very indignant. Giving the woman money enough to pay her stage-fare in returning home to a neighboring town, he commenced a suit against the dishonest agent. In addressing the jury, to whom the case was committed, he set forth in eloquent words the poverty of the aged widow, and the debt the country owed to those who, like her husband, had fought for its independence. The case was decided in her favor, and Mr. Lincoln had the pleasure of seeing the agent return her a hundred dollars.

The negroes ever found in Mr. Lincoln, even at this early period of the antislavery movement, a faithful friend. A negro mother called

upon him in great anguish. Her story was
this: She and her family were brought by her
master from Kentucky into Illinois, and set free.
Her oldest son, upon whom she was dependent,
had gone down the Mississippi on a steamboat
as a waiter. On his arrival at New Orleans he
unwisely went ashore, and was arrested and
thrown into prison, for no reason, except that
he was a free negro from a non-slaveholding
state. This outrage was further aggravated by
a threatened sale into slavery to pay his jail
expenses. The feelings of Mr. Lincoln were
aroused. He went at once to the governor,
to inquire if he could render any official aid to
the young man. The governor replied that he
was sorry to say that he could do nothing.
The powerful passions of Mr. Lincoln lost their
usual restraint, and found expression in language he seldom used. He declared he would
have the negro back or have a twenty years'
agitation in Illinois; the people should be stirred
up until the governor was invested with constitutional authority in such matters.

But it was well for the young colored man that he was not compelled to wait the results of a twenty years' agitation. Upon a sober second thought, Mr. Lincoln and his partner made up a purse and sent it to a New Orleans correspondent, who procured the negro's release and returned him to his mother.

Defending those who had been engaged in helping negroes to escape from their oppressors was a very unpopular service, not only in Illinois, but in all the states. Those lawyers especially who sought office at the hands of the politicians kept clear of so ruinous a business. A distinguished lawyer in Mr. Lincoln's own neighborhood, who has since occupied a prominent place before the country, candidly declared that he could not afford such benevolence. But an earnest worker on "the underground railroad" used to say to those needing such aid, "Go to Abraham Lincoln. He's not afraid of an unpopular case. Other lawyers may refuse, but if he is at home he will help you."

Mr. Lincoln was defending a man who was

sued for fraud in delivering to a purchaser a
number of sheep. He had agreed to deliver
those of a certain age only, but was accused
of shuffling off in the stipulated number many
much younger. In the course of the examination Mr. Lincoln became convinced that his client
had actually done as he was accused. Instead
of further attempts to prove his innocence, he
immediately confined his efforts to ascertaining
how many had been so returned, thus determin-
ing the real damage.

At another time he was conducting a prosecution against a railroad company, and succeeded in getting a decision in favor of his
client for the amount claimed, after the deduction of a certain sum which he had agreed
should be thrown off. When the judge was
about to make the final settlement, Mr. Lincoln
arose and remarked that his opponents had not
proved all that could be proved on their side,
and he then proceeded to argue against his client for a further deduction due in equity, and
the case was thus settled.

Years afterward, when the lawyers and judges with whom he was associated stood up before a great assembly of weeping citizens to pronounce Mr. Lincoln's eulogy, they remembered these rare excellences, and spoke of him with sincere and eloquent words.

.

CHAPTER XV.

AT HIS OWN HOME.

WE have followed the history of Mr. Lincoln to the year 1842. He was now thirty-three years of age; he was well established in his profession, and had risen from poverty to an income which placed him at least in circumstances of independence. He had earned an extensive reputation as a lawyer, a politician, and public speaker. Now, perhaps for the first time, he felt that his position would warrant him in getting a home of his own. He was married in November, 1842, to Miss Mary Todd, of Lexington, Ky., but at this time residing in Springfield. His nature turned fondly to the domestic circle, and his loving heart found happiness around his own hearthstone. The following letter written at this time to a friend, shows how congenial was his new relation:

" We are not keeping house, but boarding at
the Globe Tavern, which is very well kept now
by a widow of the name of Beck. Our rooms
are the same Dr. Wallace occupied there, and
boarding only costs four dollars a week. . . .
I must heartily wish you and your Fanny will
not fail to come. Just let us know the time, a
week in advance, and we will have a room
prepared for you, and we'll all be merry together for a while."

In February preceding his marriage he thus
writes to another intimate friend:

"Yours of the 16th, announcing that you
and Miss —— are no longer twain, but one flesh,
reached me this morning. I have no way of telling you how much happiness I wish you both,
though I believe you both can conceive it. I feel
somewhat jealous of both of you now, for you will
be so exclusively concerned for one another
that I shall be forgotten entirely. My acquaintance with Miss —— was too short for me to reasonably hope to be remembered by her; and still

I am sure I shall not soon forget her. Try if you cannot remind her of that debt she owes me, and be sure you do not interfere to prevent her paying it.

"I regret to learn that you have resolved not to return to Illinois. I shall be very lonesome without you. How miserably things seem to be arranged in this world! If we have no friends we have no pleasure; and if we have them we are sure to lose them, and to be doubly pained by the loss. I did hope that she and you would make your home here, yet I own I have no right to insist. You owe obligations to her ten thousand times more sacred than you can owe to others, and in that light let them be respected and observed. It is natural that you should desire to remain with her relations and friends. As to friends, *she* could not need them anywhere; she would have them in abundance here. Give my kind regards to Mr. —— and his family, particularly to Miss E.; also to your mother, brothers, and sisters. Ask little E. D. if she will ride to

town with me when I come there again.   And
finally, give a double reciprocation of all the
love she sent me.   Write me often, and believe
me yours forever,   " LINCOLN."

This playful feeling was largely manifested
in later years toward his family, especially when
his heart's warm affection became absorbed in
his children.   These were four, all sons; Robert
Todd, who has become known to the country as
an officer in its service under General Grant;
Edward, who died in infancy; William, whose
death will be more particularly noticed in
another chapter; and Thomas.   The love of
Mr. Lincoln for his children was indulged to
weakness.   When the youngest was in his arms,
and before he had received a name, he fondly
called him " Tadpole."   This was afterward
shortened to " Tad," and by that name he has
ever been known.   When his children did
wrong his chiding seldom assumed a greater
severity than the exclamation, " O, you break
my heart when you act like this ! "   But this

love and grief, manifested in his tone and countenance, were powerful in causing penitence and reformation in the erring child.

A man who lived in Springfield when a school-boy, at an early period of Mr. Lincoln's family history, gives an interesting reminiscence of his parental affection. His way to school led by Mr. Lincoln's door, and almost every fair day he saw him on the sidewalk in front of his house, hatless and coatless, and with shoes of the roughtest kind, dragging his little one to and fro in a child's carriage. His hands lay upon his back, holding the carriage, and his head and shoulders were bent forward as he strode along, seeming, as was doubtless the case, to be revolving in his mind some great subject. The school-boy looked on with interest, wondering how so rough a man happened to live in so fine a house.

Mr. Lincoln loved children wherever he met them. The pastor, at this period, of the Methodist Episcopal Church in Springfield, says that he recollects seeing Mr. Lincoln stop, as

Dragging the Wagon.

he was passing the parsonage, and toss pennies to his children who were playing in the yard, seeming to enjoy heartily their glee in picking them up.

It was quite a habit with Mr. Lincoln at this time to be lost in thought. While at his own table he would, not unfrequently, seem lost to the fact that the food was going into his mouth; and, when his current of thought was arrested, and his mind came back to his situation, he would in a pleasant manner quote a familiar piece of poetry, or a line or two from a favorite author, thus making a good retreat from his awkward position.

Sometimes Mr. Lincoln passed a familiar friend in the street with a very vacant look of recognition, if indeed he noticed him at all. When stopped and aroused from his absorbing revery, he would exclaim, "O, excuse me, I have been *thinking!*" He would then proceed to unfold a train of close thought upon some great national subject.

Mr. Lincoln enjoyed giving his family a

pleasant surprise, and he entered fully into their gladness when they thus surprised him. Once, while he was for a considerable time away upon his circuit, Mrs. Lincoln had an important alteration made in their house. He enjoyed telling the story in his own humorous way. "When I returned," he said, "I started from the depot to go to Mrs. Lincoln's; but I couldn't find it. I looked around, thinking I knew where she lived, but I could not see the place. Finally I inquired of some one, 'Can you tell me where Mrs. Lincoln lives? and he pointed the house out to me."

Whenever his public duties allowed, especially at the intervals of his holding office, Mr. Lincoln applied his mind to the acquirement of some new branch of knowledge. As he became more acquainted with men of learning, and as he was pushed forward by the people into places of greater responsibility, he felt more keenly his want of early educational advantages. Under this prompting he no doubt became better educated, in every true sense, than most gradnates of college. His remarkable memory, which retained in detail what he had learned, and his clear understanding of every subject, gave him an advantage in the pursuit of knowledge over the mass of even studious men. His privileges were small, but his mental capacity was great. He did not come before the public, even in his earliest offices, an ignorant man, but a very intelligent one, especially in regard to the duties he was expected to perform.

In his early professional career he began the study of geometry. He had often heard in discussions the word "demonstrate," and he determined to understand it fully. He persevered until he could "demonstrate" promptly any proposition of the first six books of Euclid. He is said to have learned mathematics with great facility, and he might perhaps have become distinguished in this branch of study under favoring circumstances.

Mr. Lincoln early manifested a mechanical taste. He not only built log-cabins and flatboats, but other useful things requiring more skill. During some months of leisure, after he became the head of a family, he diverted himself in endeavoring to invent an attachment for the bottom of the steamboats of the western rivers, which should buoy them up in shoal water. He produced something which he thought would answer. It was a kind of bellows, which, when fastened to the bottom, could be filled with air or emptied as required. By this means he thought that the vessel might avoid the danger of sudden changes in the depth of the water. A rough model, which seemed in part to be "whittled" out, was sent to Washington and a patent obtained. The model may now be seen in the Patent Office, but we have not heard that the invention was ever tried upon the bottom of a steamboat.

At a later period he wrote a lecture upon inventions, giving their history from him "who was the father of all such as handle the harp and organ," and from him "who was an instructor of every artificer in brass and iron" to the latest inventor of "a Yankee notion." The lecture was read in public twice, and then followed his invention into obscurity.

While thus busy with inventions and study, Mr. Lincoln did not entirely neglect more serious concerns. His wife being a member of the Presbyterian Church, he sat under the ministry of that denomination. He contributed cheerfully, and, according to his means, liberally, to the institutions and benevolent operations of the Church. His law partner, with whom he commenced business in 1844, says that he was then a good biblical scholar.

This partner, who observed Mr. Lincoln closely for many years, says of his character, as he appeared to him at this time: "He approached more nearly the angelic nature than any person I had ever seen, woman not excepted. He had an angel-looking eye and face; yet he was not without passions. These in Lincoln were powerful, but they were under the control of a giant will. He had a towering ambition, but that ambition was directed for the attainment of power with which to elevate man."

We shall not be surprised, after these glances at Mr. Lincoln at home and among his neighbors, and after having their estimate of him, to follow him into the halls of Congress.

CHAPTER XVI.

IN CONGRESS.

Such had been Mr. Lincoln's popularity with his party that he felt warranted in expecting the nomination to Congress, which took place soon after his marriage. But the convention of his county to appoint delegates to the district nominating convention, sent him a delegate, under instructions to vote for the nomination of another man. This disappointment he bore with his accustomed good-nature. He wrote to a friend, saying: "In getting Baker the nomination, I shall be fixed a good deal like a fellow that is made groomsman to the man who has cut him out, and is marrying his own dear gal." When his rival was nominated, he supported him with sincerity and zeal.

When Henry Clay received the nomination of the Whig party as their candidate for the presidency, Mr. Lincoln entered at once into the efforts for his success in Illinois. He lectured in every part of the state, and did the party and their candidate great service by his able statements and defense of their principles. He even extended his itinerating for this purpose into Indiana. He had indulged, not only in the sincere conviction that Mr. Clay would make a better president than his rival, but in the confident hope of his election. When, therefore, he learned that the people of the country had decided otherwise, he retired for a time from the political field with feelings of discouragement, if not of disgust. His estimate of Mr. Clay had been formed in boyhood, in part at least, by the reading of his life, and in his imagination the great orator occupied a position of dazzling pre-eminence among common statesmen.

Mr. Lincoln's electioneering, though it had failed in its particular objects, secured results which he least sought: it greatly increased his own reputation as a sound thinker, a true statesman, and an able and fair debater. It also incidentally showed that he was a man of true courage. His low estimate of himself, and his uniform readiness to give way to the claims of others, had led those who could not understand real greatness to esteem him a timid man. A personal friend of Mr. Lincoln had made a speech of great eloquence and power, which excited the anger of the opposing party, and some of them declared he should not speak again. Hearing the threats, Mr. Lincoln and Col. Baker, afterward the distinguished senator from Oregon, took their seats at his side the next time he addressed the people, and when he had finished, quietly walked with him to his hotel. " The boys" knew the men, and concluded that prudence was the safest policy.

Mr. Lincoln subsequently defended Col. Baker in a manner amusing as well as heroic. Baker was speaking with great enthusiasm, and, in the midst of his zeal, uttered some expressions which called forth the wrath of his political enemies. " Take him out !" shouted several voices. "Yes, pull him down," responded others, and the mob were getting furious. Instantly Mr. Lincoln dropped, apparently through the ceiling, and landed at the side of his friend. He had been listening, unseen by the audience, at an old scuttle, directly over the speaker's stand. Hearing the mutterings of the storm below, he appeared to stem its rage. "Gentlemen," said he, "let us not disgrace the age and country in which we live. Baker has a right to speak, and ought to be permitted to do so. I am here to protect him, and no man shall take him from this stand if I can prevent it."

The calm attitude of Mr. Lincoln, while uttering these words gave assurance that he was in earnest, and Col. Baker finished without further interruption.

Mr. Lincoln was not left long in retirement after the Clay campaign. In 1847 he received the Whig nomination to represent "the Sangamon district" in Congress. He had desired this honor, but was too noble-minded to stoop to political trickery to obtain it. He was ambitious to secure a seat in the national legislature, but his desire did not spring from a selfish purpose, nor did he have in view a low end. He felt conscious of the noble powers God had given him, and wished to use them for the good of men.

His election proved his popularity. He received a vote much larger than that which his party commanded at other times.

He took his seat in Congress December 6, 1847. He had seen enough of public life to be able to feel at home in this new position. He appeared before the House several times during the winter in speeches upon questions in debate. There were great men there, among whom were John Quincy Adams, Robert Winthrop, Alexander Stevens, and N. P. Banks. But the new representative from the West always commanded attention when he spoke. He was master of his subject when he rose, and he uttered his thoughts in clear, forcible language, often made sparkling by a sharp

retort, an apt illustration, or a witty compari-
son.   His bearing had the same unaffected
simplicity that it did among the people of the
Illinois log-cabins.   On one occasion, wishing
to take some law books from the capitol to his
boarding-house for the purpose of examining a
subject then in discussion, he put them in a silk
handkerchief, and was proceeding to tie them
up.   A friend observing this, remarked, "Mr.
Lincoln, I wouldn't trouble myself in that
way; send for a messenger-boy to carry them."

"O no," replied Mr. Lincoln coolly; "I'll
carry them myself, and then I shall know they
are there in time."

So having tied the corners of the handkerchief, he run his cane under the knot, and,
swinging his books over his shoulder, marched
as unconcernedly through the streets of Washington to his hotel as if he had been on his
western law circuit.

While in Washington Mr. Lincoln was true
to the antislavery principles he so nobly defended in the Illinois legislature, and in his

speeches before the people. He voted with such men as John Quincy Adams, Mr. Wilmot, and Joshua R. Giddings, for free speech on the subject of slavery, and for such legislation on that vexed matter as he considered constitutional. The antislavery views and measures he then adopted appear very far from the standard of the present time, but he was in advance of the majority of his contemporaries in what he was willing to do and suffer in the cause of the slave.

When Mr. Lincoln's term of service in Congress was closed he made a brief tour in New England, delivering a few political speeches. He then returned home, and continued his public addresses in his own state. His long absence from his private business had of course injured it, and, no doubt, continued public service would have been agreeable to him. But there were other aspirants of his own party for his seat in Congress, and the nomination was given to one of them, whose defeat at the polls proved that Mr. Lincoln's own popularity,

and not the strength of the party, had given
him the previous election. Though he doubtless believed he possessed this popularity, he
was too high-minded to press his own claims
when other friends of the cause were put
forward.

After General Taylor was nominated for the
presidency, Mr. Lincoln spent much time in
advocating his claims as a candidate; and when
the general had become president, he made
some efforts through friends to obtain the responsible position of Commissioner of the
General Land Office. He did not, however,
get the appointment, and he used afterward to
make himself very merry over the effort and its
failure.

CHAPTER XVII.

A GREAT CONTEST COMMENCED.

AFTER leaving Congress Mr. Lincoln attended closely to his law business for nearly five years. The following incident, which occurred near the close of this period, that is, in the early part of 1854, illustrates the pleasing fact that the bad influences at Washington had not shaken his temperance habits.

The Illinois legislature were making a three days' excursion to Chicago, Mr. Lincoln being a special guest of the party. During the upward trip the party were sufficiently noisy, especially at the stopping-places, where the political leaders were called out in brief speeches; but the feasting and toasting by the knowing ones of Chicago, who desired votes from the legislators for a particular law, did not improve either their speech or manners. On the return

10

trip half of the best speakers had given out "with fatigue, or something else," and others were filling their friends with shame when they attempted to speak. From the commencement of the excursion the people when calling for speakers never omitted the name of Lincoln, and when he appeared on the platform the wildest shouts rent the air, and the passengers in the cars would pass along the remark, "There, hear that! Abe has been telling one of his good yarns. What a fellow he is! He carries the people off their feet." As the party approached the termination of their excursion there seemed but one name shouted at every stopping-place, and that was "Lincoln! Lincoln!" His tall form was more erect, and his voice rung out with a fuller, clearer tone than at the beginning. The spirit of his speeches may be learned from the following remarks dropped by one of the members to his wife: "Abe is talking temperance. How he does lash the drinking rascals! There are not ten duly sober men in the whole crowd; not one

but himself but has drank some. No persua-
sion, no influence which could be brought to
bear, has induced him to touch anything but
cold water; and while all the rest are sick,
tired out, and wholly used up, he is as fresh
as when we started, the noblest Illinoisian of
us all."

In 1854 a law was made by Congress, by
which slaves might be permitted to go into the
new territories if the voters so wished; but
the slaveholders and their friends intended to
take advantage of this law, and *force* slavery upon Kansas, and into all the currents of
western emigration. This act aroused Mr.
Lincoln, and his life-long hatred of slavery
burned with fresh intensity. He had been
quiet, wishing perhaps to see what could be
done by those who were determined to impose
silence upon lawmakers respecting the peculiar
institution. But he now saw that when the
enemies of slavery submitted to an imposed
silence, the slaveholders were the most active
in extending it.

The author of this law, which so moved Mr.
Lincoln, was Stephen A. Douglas, a senator
from his own state. Mr. Douglas had come to
Illinois from Vermont when a young man, and
first met Mr. Lincoln in the state legislature.
In most respects they were extremely unlike.
Mr. Lincoln was the tallest man of the house,
and remarkable for bodily strength. Mr.
Douglas was the smallest as well as the youngest member, and of slight frame. Mr. Lincoln
was modest, distrustful of his own abilities, and
confident only when he had tried and succeeded, knowing and feeling his want of early
education and lack of attractive personal presence. Mr. Douglas won his way by an easy
address, and a confidence in himself which
never failed him, though in the presence of the
great, or in competition with men of large experience and high position. Mr. Douglas was
made a judge at a very early age, and when
Mr. Lincoln entered Congress as a representative, his competitor took his seat in the more
honorable place of United States senator.

Now, when the two were about to come before the country as opponents on the subject of slavery, Mr. Douglas had become the strongest party leader of the West, if not of the United States. His word commanded universal attention, and, with his political friends, well-nigh universal assent. But his new move for slavery had strengthened the opposition of his enemies, and weakened the attachment of his friends. On the adjournment of the Congress in which it was made, he turned his face toward home, moving slowly, like a truant boy who fears to meet the frowns of a justly offended father. When he arrived at Chicago, and attempted boldly to defend his course, the excited people were loud in their denunciations, and refused to hear him. This was not the treatment that Mr. Lincoln desired to have him receive, and when Mr. Douglas came to Springfield a few weeks afterward, where a state fair was being held, and a great multitude of people were assembled from all parts of the state, no man listened more closely to his lengthy speech than he. He not only *listened* to it, but he understood it and the whole subject in all its bearings. The next day he stood up before that multitude, and replied to it in a speech three hours long.

This speech is thus described by one present : "Mr. Lincoln quivered with feeling and emotion. The whole house was as still as death. He attacked the bill with unusual warmth and energy, and all felt that a man of strength was its enemy, and that he intended to blast it if he could by strong and manly efforts. He was most successful, and the house approved the glorious triumph of truth by loud and long-continued huzzas. Women waved their white handkerchiefs in token of woman's silent but heartfelt consent. . . . Mr. Lincoln exhibited Douglas in all the attitudes in which he could be placed in a friendly debate. He exhibited the bill in all its aspects, to show its humbuggery and falsehood, and when thus torn to rags, cut into slips, and held up to the gaze of the vast crowd, a kind of scorn was visible upon the face of the crowd and upon the lips of the most eloquent speaker. . . . At the conclusion of the speech every man felt that it was unanswerable; that no human power could overthrow it or trample it under foot. The long and repeated applause evinced the feelings of the crowd, and gave token of universal assent to Lincoln's whole argument; and every mind present did homage to the man who took captive the heart, and broke like a sun over the understanding."

When Mr. Lincoln sat down, Mr. Douglas sprang to his feet to reply. His boldness was much abated, for he saw that the confidence of the people in the justness of his bill was gone. He talked for a short time, and then claimed the right of continuing his remarks in the evening. This right was conceded to him, but he failed to appear. "The Little Giant" arose to conquer as at other times, but his strength was gone.

Mr. Douglas spoke a few days after at Peoria. Mr. Lincoln had followed him, and he replied to his speech in such a manner that no answer was attempted.   Mr. Douglas had received enough of his earnest, honest opponent's "replies;" they proved *answers* which allowed of no "answering again," and it is reported that he requested Mr. Lincoln not again to challenge him to debate.   It is certain that for a while they both went their way to speak in different places.   Mr. Lincoln's speeches in these few discussions were like unexpected shots thrown into an enemy's camp, creating confusion and some fear, but leaving a fierce determination to "fight it out."   The old political parties became more and more feeble, some from the ranks of both combining against them for the sake of the bondman.

In 1856 Mr. Lincoln finally broke away from the political organization to which he had been much attached, and for which he had spent much time and given his great influence, and became one of the organizers of a republican party in Illinois.   This step gave increased force to his denunciations of slavery.   He made a speech at the first convention of the party, which was full of argument and fiery eloquence. It was thus noticed at the time : "Never was an audience more completely electrified by human eloquence. Again and again, during the progress of its delivery, they sprang to their feet and upon the benches, and testified by long-continued shouts and the waving of hats how deeply the speaker had wrought upon their minds and hearts. It fused the mass of the hitherto incongruous elements into perfect homogeneity, and from that day they worked together in harmonious and fraternal union." Mr. Lincoln became at once the western leader of the new party, and in making up their ticket for the presidential election of 1856, he was extensively named for the second place on it, which was finally given to Judge Dayton. This showed the esteem in which he was then held where he had become well known, and pointed significantly toward the White House, though there was to be, before entering it, an achievement of a triumph on an important field of conflict.

CHAPTER XVIII.

A TRIUMPH ACHIEVED.

IN 1858 a new and more exciting turn was given to the antislavery controversy. Judge Douglas's law in favor of what he called "popular sovereignty," professing to let the people of the new states vote slavery "up or down," had resulted in forcing, by fraud, a slaveholder's constitution upon Kansas. Douglas opposed the *fraud*, but still defended the law which occasioned it. Lincoln insisted in his speeches that the law itself was a cheat. This led to a famous controversy between these two great men, by which the fame of both was extended, and by which slavery and freedom were held up in a clearer light to the gaze of the people.

It happened that Douglas's term of service in the United States Senate expired about this time. The convention of his party met in

April and nominated him as their candidate for another term. The Republican party met in June, and nominated Mr. Lincoln for the same office. The two candidates commenced at once to address the people concerning the questions upon which they differed, the principal one being slavery. The good temper in which this controversy was carried on was very remarkable. The disputants began with a kind word for each other. Mr. Lincoln thus spoke of Judge Douglas: "Twenty-two years ago Judge Douglas and I first became acquainted. We were both young then, he a trifle younger than I. Even then we were both ambitious, I perhaps quite as much so as he. With me the race of ambition has been a failure, a flat failure; with him it has been one of splendid success. His name fills the nation, and is not unknown even in foreign lands. I affect no contempt for the high eminence he has reached. So reached that the oppressed of my species might have shared with me in the elevation, I would rather stand on that eminence than wear the richest crown that ever pressed a monarch's brow." Mr. Lincoln, in a speech early in the campaign, thus playfully alludes to the advantages his opponent had over him in the minds of many influential persons, who were expecting his nomination for the presidential office : " They have seen in his round, jolly, fruitful face, post-offices, land-offices, marshalships, and cabinet appointments, chargeships, and foreign missions bursting and sprouting out in wonderful luxuriance, ready to be laid hold of by their greedy hands. And as they have been gazing upon this attractive picture so long, they cannot, in the little distraction that has taken place in the party, bring themselves to give up the charming hope ; but with greedier anxiety they rush about him, sustain him, give him marches, triumphal entries, and receptions, beyond what even in the days of his highest prosperity they could have brought about in his favor. On the contrary, nobody has ever expected me to be president. In my poor, lean, lank face nobody has ever seen that any cabbages were sprouting out."

Mr. Douglas refers in the following manner to Mr. Lincoln : " I take great pleasure in saying that I have known personally and intimately the worthy gentleman who has been nominated for my place, and I will say that I regard him as a kind, amiable, and intelligent man, a good citizen, and an honorable opponent ; and whatever issues I may have with him will be of principles and not of personalities."

Mr. Lincoln made his first speech of this famous senatorial campaign at Springfield, Illinois, to the convention of a thousand delegates which nominated him, and to the crowd which gathered with them.   It was carefully prepared, every sentence being guarded and emphatic. Before entering the hall where it was to be delivered, he stepped into the office of his law-partner, Mr. Herndon, and locking the door, that their interview might be strictly private, took the manuscript from his pocket and read the opening statement, which was that " this government cannot endure permanently half slave and half free."   Mr. Herndon remarked that the sentiment was true, but suggested that it might not be good *policy* to utter it at that time. Mr. Lincoln replied with great firmness: "No matter about the *policy*. It is *true*, and the nation is entitled to it. The proposition has been true for six thousand years, and I will deliver it as it is written."

This speech made a deep impression, not only from the zeal and evident sincerity of the speaker, but from the sound argument presented.

Soon after, Mr. Douglas went to Chicago, where the first excitement concerning his late course in the Senate had prevented his speaking. His friends now rallied, and a very flattering reception was given to him. Cheers greeted his appearance upon the platform, and constant cheering stimulated his desperate determination to talk down the rising popular feeling which threatened to sweep away both his office and influence. The effect of his speech showed that if his power over the masses was waning, it was still great. No man could have done better with so bad a cause. It was evident that he who should dare follow him would be a bold man.

Mr. Lincoln had listened to Mr. Douglas, and fully understood every argument and every evasion, and the next evening he took the stand, greeted by deafening applause. Although his opponent had been provoking in his treatment of his Springfield speech, he was in excellent humor while showing this unfairness. He used the occasion to reaffirm his sentiments concerning slavery. He said: "I have always hated slavery, I trust, as much as any Abolitionist. I have been an Old Line Whig. I have always hated it, but I have been quiet about it until this new era of the introduction of the Nebraska bill began. I have always believed that everybody was against it, and that it was in course of ultimate extinction."

So clear were his statements, and so plainly honest every word, that the mass of the people who heard him were evidently brought into full sympathy with his political doctrines.

Mr. Douglas made no reply, but went to other parts of the state, followed by his opponent, with his annoying popularity and his more annoying arguments. Mr. Lincoln even proposed to Mr. Douglas that they should travel through the state together, agreeing upon some plan of discussion at every point. This Mr. Douglas declined, but after some delay, during which they spoke in different places, he agreed that they should hold public discussions in seven prominent towns. The arrangements in reference to this proposal were made and carried out. Mr. Douglas, being rich, is said to have traveled with great parade, spending many thousands of dollars during the discussion. Mr. Lincoln maintained his usual simplicity, and very innocently remarked at the close, that it had been a very expensive work, and he really thought it had cost him five hundred dollars. But sometimes the two opponents traveled together in friendly chat in the same carriage or public conveyance.

The magazines and journals of the day contained reports of the debate, and graphic pen-portraits of the disputants, of which the following is a good example : "During this political contest with Mr. Douglas, Mr. Lincoln not only proved himself an able speaker and a good tactician, but demonstrated that it is possible to carry on the fiercest political warfare without once descending to rude personality and coarse denunciation. We have it on the authority of a person who followed Abraham Lincoln throughout the whole of that campaign, that, in spite of all the temptations to an opposite course to which he was continually exposed, no personalities against his opponent, no vituperations or coarseness, ever defiled his lips. His kind and genial nature lifted him above a resort to any such weapon of political warfare, and it was the commonly expressed regret of fiercer natures that he treated his opponent so courteously and urbanely. Vulgar personalities and vituperation are the last things that can be truthfully charged against Abraham Lincoln. His heart is too genial, his good

11

sense too strong, and his innate self-respect too predominant to permit him to indulge in them. His nobility of nature, and we use the term advisedly, has been as steadfast throughout his whole career as his temperate habits, his self-reliance, and his intellectual power."

Another writer thus sketches both the debaters as they appeared in their discussion at Galesburgh: "The men are entirely dissimilar. Mr. Douglas is a thick-set, finely-built, courageous man, and has an air of self-confidence that does not a little to inspire his supporters with hope. Mr. Lincoln is a tall, lank man, awkward, apparently diffident, and, when not speaking, has not firmness in his countenance nor fire in his eye. He has a rich silvery voice; he enunciates with great distinctness, and has a fine command of language.

"Mr. Lincoln commenced by a review of the points Mr. Douglass had made. In this he showed great tact, and his retorts, though gentlemanly, were sharp, and reached to the core the subject in dispute. While he gave but

little time to the work of review, we did not
feel that anything was omitted which deserved
attention.

"He then proceeded to defend the Republican party. Here he charged Mr. Douglas
with doing nothing for freedom; with disre-
garding the rights and interests of the colored
man; and for about forty minutes he spoke
with a power that we have seldom heard
equaled. There was a grandeur in his
thoughts, a comprehensiveness in his arguments, and a binding force in his conclusions,
which were perfectly irresistible. The vast
throng was silent as death; every eye was fixed
upon the speaker, and all gave him serious
attention. He was the tall man eloquent; his
countenance glowed with animation, and his
eye glistened with an intelligence that made it
lustrous. He was no longer awkward and
ungainly, but graceful, bold, and commanding.

"Mr. Douglas had been quietly smoking up
to this time; but here he forgot his cigar, and
listened with anxious attention. When he rose

to reply, he appeared excited, disturbed, and his second effort seemed to us vastly inferior to his first. Mr. Lincoln had given a great talk, and he had neither time nor ability to answer him."

The eyes of the whole country were turned toward Illinois, and the debaters were followed from point to point through the reports of the public journals. When the debate was closed the Republican party published the speeches of both, without alteration or comment, and scattered them over the country, greatly swelling the wave of influence which soon changed the administration of the general government.

Mr. Lincoln's reputation as a great and good man was immensely advanced; but he lost, and Mr. Douglas won, the position of United States senator, by the vote of their state legislature. If the people of the state had voted *directly* on the question, instead of by their representatives, they would have given Mr. Lincoln a majority of four thousand.

When Mr. Lincoln was asked how he felt

when he learned that he had been defeated, he replied: "Like the boy who struck his toe against a stone, too much hurt to laugh, and too big to cry."

But he had convinced the people of his own state, and had done much to convince the mass of the people in all the free states, that his *principles*, the principles of universal freedom, were right. This was achieving a triumph which bore him beyond the senatorship to a position from which the White House was clearly in view.

CHAPTER XIX.

THE WHITE HOUSE IN PROSPECT.

THE interest of the people of the United States in the presidential election which was to take place in November, 1860, commenced its significant manifestation many months previous. The cries of the oppressed negroes of the South had entered the ears of God, and he had given to many thousands of the voters hearts to feel their wrongs. Men in every part of the free states were saying, Slavery shall extend no further; our new territories which are now free shall never be polluted by the feet of slaveholders, with their property in men and women; we cannot touch it in the states where it now exists, but there it shall stay until its own wicked and hated character shall kill it.

We have seen that Mr. Lincoln had been in the West an honest and earnest standard-bearer for those who held these sentiments, so that the very first movements in that section of the country toward selecting a candidate for the presidential office gave evidence that the thoughts and hearts of the people were turned to him. But men have sometimes very boyish and very foolish ways of showing their interest in serious and important matters. They called General Jackson " Old Hickory," and made a great cry about his being like the "gnarled oak" when politicians wished to twist him about; they made a great noise concerning log-cabins and hard cider when General Harrison was a presidential candidate; and now, when they wished to bring Mr. Lincoln into notice for the same high office, many men seemed to think that there must be some such rallying cry in order to elect him. Doubtless all these good and great men were mortified to have their names connected with such foolish matters, which had nothing to do with their fitness for the honorable and difficult duties of president of a great nation.

The key-note of this kind of party watch-word was given by Mr. Lincoln's friends in his own state, and early in the campaign. In May, 1859, the Illinois state republican convention met in Decatur, and Mr. Lincoln attended as a spectator. When he entered the hall a burst of applause greeted him, which seemed to shake the foundation of the building. The sight of his homely but honest face, so expressive of intelligence and power, electrified the audience. He had hardly taken his seat when the governor of the state arose, and said that an old democrat wished to make a presentation to the convention. Permission being given, two old fence-rails were borne into the hall, covered with showy decorations. They bore the inscription, " Abraham Lincoln, the rail candidate for the presidency in 1860. Two rails from a lot of three thousand, made in 1830 by Thomas Hanks and Abe Lincoln, whose father was the first pioneer of Macon County."

At sight of these emblems of their favorite's popular character and humble origin, the ex-

cited crowd sprang to their feet, and showed
their enthusiasm by vociferous and long continued cheering. When at last the tumult had
in a measure subsided, Mr. Lincoln was called
upon to explain the statement respecting the
rails. This he did by modestly rehearsing the
facts, which we have given in their place in his
history, relating to his breaking up some land
for his father, and splitting rails to inclose it.
The shouts of "The rail-splitter of Illinois the
people's choice for the presidency," were taken
up by the hardy tillers of the soil in every part
of the great West, and were echoed from the
far off Atlantic and Pacific shores. The noisy
demonstration of the people did not affect Mr.
Lincoln, except as they gave evidence of an
increasing love for the cause of the oppressed.
He was busy with the great principles of universal freedom, convincing the masses by his
strong arguments, and winning their hearts by
his kind spirit.

He visited Kansas, and the people greeted his
coming among them with an enthusiastic wel-

come both universal and sincere. No conqueror, returning with the trophies of his victory, could have so taken captive all hearts. They remembered his generous words and deeds in their behalf during their dark days of brave but unequal contest with the slave power.

After visiting Kansas, Mr. Lincoln followed Judge Douglas into Ohio, repeating and enlarging upon the arguments of the great senatorial discussion. He spoke at Cincinnati to immense crowds, uttering many kind and wise words for the slaveholders across the river, knowing that the papers along the border would publish his speech.

In the early part of 1860 Mr. Lincoln turned his face toward the Atlantic states. He had not yet become known much out of the West, except by the report of his debates with Judge Douglas. He had received an invitation to speak in the Rev. Henry Ward Beecher's church in Brooklyn. He accepted the invitation, and on the twenty-fifth of February arrived in New York. After reaching the Astor House on Saturday, he learned, to his surprise, that arrangements had been made by his political friends for him to speak in the Cooper Institute of the great metropolis. When visited by the great men of his party, he was found dressed in a new suit of black, badly wrinkled by being closely packed in his valise. He felt embarrassed by his unbecoming dress, as well as by his new and, to him, strange position, and spoke of both to his visitors with a childlike simplicity.

Having on Saturday reviewed and modified his speech with reference to the change of place of its delivery, he attended, with evident satisfaction, Mr. Beecher's church on Sunday. On Monday he was taken by his friends through some of the principal streets and largest business establishments of the city. He met, while looking at its wonderful things, an old friend from Illinois, who remarked, in the course of their conversation, that he had made and lost since coming to New York a hundred thousand dollars, and, looking earnestly at Mr. Lincoln, added, "And how is it with you?" "O very well," he replied. "I have the cottage in Springfield, and about eight thousand dollars in money. If they make me vice-president with Seward, as some say they will, I hope I shall be able to increase it to twenty thousand, and that is as much as any man ought to want."

He met, at a photograph establishment, George Bancroft, the famous and learned historian. He felt embarrassed when introduced to one of such eminent refinement, but still he maintained his natural frankness and freedom of conversation. He told Mr. Bancroft that he was going to Cambridge, in Massachusetts, where he had a son who, if reports were true, already knew more than his father.

Mr. Lincoln felt a burden upon his spirits as he returned to his hotel. He was to speak that night to one of the largest and most intelligent audiences that ever assembled in the country. His excursion during the day had painfully impressed him with a sense of his own insignificance. He was ambitious, but distrustful of his abilities. He knew he had succeeded in speaking to his own people in the West, to whom he thought his peculiar manner might be adapted. But would the people who were accustomed to hear the most scholarly and able men of the country listen to him with favor?

Such were some of the thoughts with which Mr. Lincoln entered the hall of the institute. He found it crowded with gentlemen and ladies, who had an intense curiosity to hear him. The platform was occupied by the distinguished men of the Republican party of Brooklyn and New York.

Mr. Lincoln's fears concerning the reception of his speech proved entirely groundless. No one effort of his life of this kind did so much to increase his fame and influence. He said to the reporters who had called upon him for notes of his speech before its delivery, that he did not think any of the editors would consider it worth an extended notice. But it was published and read all over the free states. Men wondered at its unanswerable logic, its pure English, and happy illustrations. The forest boy of the West became the lion of the East.

After the lecture Mr. Lincoln tarried until a late hour at a supper given by his special friends, delighting them as much by his stories and good-humor in the social circle as he had surprised them by his intellectual power in public.

He spent a few days in further sight-seeing at New York. A teacher in the Five Points House of Industry relates the following incident which occurred during one of his calls:

"Our Sunday-school in the Five Points was assembled one Sabbath morning a few months since, when I noticed a tall and remarkable looking man enter the room and take a seat among us. He listened with fixed attention to our exercises, and his countenance manifested such genuine interest, that I approached him and suggested that he might be willing to say something to the children. He accepted the invitation with evident pleasure, and, coming forward, began a simple address which at once fascinated every little hearer, and hushed the room into silence. His language was strikingly beautiful, and his tones musical with intensest feeling. The little faces around would droop into sad conviction as he uttered sentences of warning, and would brighten into sunshine as he spoke cheerful words of promise. Once or twice he attempted to close his remarks, but the imperative shout of 'Go on! O do go on!' would compel him to resume. As he was quietly leaving the room I begged to know his name. He courteously replied, 'It is Abraham Lincoln, of Illinois.'"

Leaving New York, Mr. Lincoln made an excursion through some of the principal cities of Connecticut, and visited his son at Harvard College, Mass. He made speeches in several cities with great success. In New Haven a professor of rhetoric in Yale College went to hear his address, and gave a lecture the next day to his class on its excellences. The professor was so much pleased and impressed by the speaker that he followed him to Meriden to learn more concerning his wonderful originality and power.

A distinguished clergyman of Norwich, after a familiar conversation with Mr. Lincoln concerning his remarkable success as a speaker, said, as they were about to part, "Mr. Lincoln, may I say one thing to you before we separate?"

"Certainly; anything you please," was the reply.

"You have just spoken," said the minister, "of the tendency of political life in Washington to lead our representatives to act from expediency instead of principle. You have become one of our leaders in the great struggle with slavery which is *the* struggle of the nation and the age. What I would like to say is this, and I say it with a full heart: Be true to your principles and we will be true to you, and God will be true to us all." Mr. Lincoln was greatly moved by the earnestness of the appeal, and, taking his friend's extended hand in both of his own, exclaimed, "I say amen to that! Amen to that!"

During these itineratings of Mr. Lincoln, the wave of popular excitement in reference to the questions which were to enter into the approaching presidential election was plainly increasing in extent and force; and as the excitement increased the name of Abraham Lincoln became more prominent. With, therefore, the White House clearly in prospect, he returned to his Illinois home to await the result of the approaching nominating convention, and the decisive utterances of the voice of the people which were to follow.

12

CHAPTER XX.

THE VOICE OF THE PEOPLE.

IN April, 1860, the people began to speak in reference to the presidential candidates. Several conventions were held, and Stephen A. Douglas, Mr. Lincoln's old opponent, John C. Breckenridge, a slaveholder of Kentucky, and John Bell, of Tennessee, were nominated. But the convention in which the people of the free states were most interested, and toward which the eyes of the whole country were turned, met at Chicago on the sixteenth of June. It assembled in a building of immense size put up for the purpose, and called "The Wigwam." The people who had flocked to Chicago to witness or to influence the doings of the convention could hardly be numbered; fifteen hundred slept in a single hotel. All comfortable lodging places of the vast city were occupied, and many

were compelled to be content with very poor
ones.

After some debate the convention adopted
its "platform," which might be called the inscription to be put upon the republican ban-
ners and carried into every battle during the
presidential campaign.   It was antislavery and
" free soil."   When it was announced, the ex- .
citement of the people became intense.   An
eyewitness thus describes it: " All the thousands of men in that enormous wigwam commenced swinging their hats, and cheering with
intense enthusiasm; and the other thousands of
ladies waved their handkerchiefs and clapped
their hands.   The roar that went up from the
mass of ten thousand human beings is inde-
scribable.   Such a spectacle as was presented
for some minutes has never been witnessed
at a convention.   A herd of buffaloes or lions
could not have made a more tremendous
roaring."

Before the balloting for a candidate was commenced, a telegram was sent to Mr. Lincoln.   It

told him that the votes of certain two delega-
tions would decide the nomination in his favor,
and that he could have them if he would promise the chairman of each a place in his cabinet.
Promptly the wires flashed the following reply:

"I authorize no bargains, and will be bound
by none.　　　　　　　　"A. LINCOLN."

Now came the voting.　On the third balloting Abraham Lincoln received a majority.　The
painful silence which attended the voting
was succeeded by deafening shouts when the
result was announced.　Inside the wigwam the
multitude cheered until strength failed them.
A man who had been standing upon the roof
during the voting shouted the name of Abraham
Lincoln.　Cannon had been mounted on the top
of one of the hotels, and in other conspicuous
positions, and all were ready for the match.
When, therefore, the sentinel called from the
top of the wigwam, the answering guns thun-
dered their approval in every direction.　The

multitude without responded to the multitude
within, and the mingled shouts were "as the
voice of many waters."   The great city of
Chicago was wild with joy.   The dignity of
great men, and the sobriety of the aged, were
borne away in the common enthusiasm.   As
the telegraphic wires flashed over the whole
country the name of Abraham Lincoln, the
people knew what it meant.   It meant a political struggle between slavery and freedom—a
struggle for the rule of the many against the
rule of the few, such as the world had never
seen.   All the loyal, liberty-loving people rejoiced, and responded to the shouts of the great
city of the West, from every city, town, and village of the free states.

During the excitement of the voting at
Chicago, Mr. Lincoln was quietly sitting with
his friends in the office of "The Journal," at
Springfield, Illinois.   It cannot be supposed
that his interest was otherwise than intense as
the telegram conveyed to him the result of each
balloting.   When, at last, the telegram came

which announced his nomination, he took it from the hands of the messenger of the telegraph office, and read it, first in silence, and then to the friends about him. He was not exultant. It is reported that clouds of sadness were seen alternating with the expressions of joy upon his countenance. He knew well what burdens this news foreshadowed. Having waited a few moments to receive the congratulations of his friends, he quietly pocketed the telegram, saying, as he walked from the office, that there was " a little woman " at home who had an interest in the matter.

That evening Mr. Lincoln was engaged until a late hour receiving the congratulations of the citizens of Springfield, who sincerely and ardently loved him. On the next day came a committee from the Chicago Convention, bearing the official announcement of his nomination. Mr. Lincoln's Springfield friends, thinking to do him a favor, had sent to his house sundry vessels of strong drink. They thought he would need it to give a fitting reception to the eminent

men who were about to call upon him. But
this was not in accordance with his principles or
practices; being embarrassed by it, he privately
took counsel about the matter with a friend on
the committee before they came in formally.
This friend said, "Mr. Lincoln, I advise you to
return the liquor, and act in acordance with
your principles." This he did, as will be seen
in the following account given by an eyewitness.
The speech of the chairman of the committee
had been made on presenting the nomination,
and Mr. Lincoln had replied, accepting it with
expressions of distrust in himself, and of confidence in God's blessing.   .

"Mr. Lincoln then remarked to the company
that, as an appropriate conclusion to an interview so important and interesting as that which
had just transpired, he supposed good manners
would require that he should treat the committee with something to drink; and, opening a
door that led into a room in the rear, he called
out, 'Mary! Mary!' A girl responded to the
call, to whom Mr. Lincoln spoke a few words in

an undertone; and, closing the door, returned
again to converse with his guests. In a few
moments the maiden entered bearing a large
waiter containing several tumblers and a pitch-
er in the midst, and placed it upon the center-
table. Mr. Lincoln arose, and gravely addressing the company, said : ' Gentlemen, we must
pledge our mutual healths in the most healthy
beverage God has given to man ; it is the only
beverage I have ever used or allowed in my
family, and I cannot conscientiously depart
from it on the present occasion ; it is pure
Adam's ale from the spring.' Taking a tum-
bler, he touched it to his lips and pledged them
his highest respects in a cup of cold water. Of
course all his guests were constrained to admit
his consistency and join in his example."

The committee, though not merry with wine,
were very cheerful. Judge Kelley, of Pennsylvania, a very tall man, as he approached to
shake hands with Mr. Lincoln, paused, and in a
pleasant manner looked at him from head to
foot, as if about to estimate his height. Mr.

Lincoln observed this, and, as he took the judge's hand, said,

"Judge, how high are you?"

"Six feet three," replied the judge. "What is your height, Mr. Lincoln?"

"Six feet four," answered Mr. Lincoln.

"Then, sir," said the judge, "Pennsylvania bows to Illinois. My dear man," he added, "for many years my heart has been aching for a president I could look up to, and I've found him at last in the land where we thought there were none but LITTLE giants."

Mr. Lincoln, being now regarded as the property of the nation, was allowed to have no rest at his own home. The sudden increase of his friends was truly wonderful. With unfaltering patience he gave attention to each visitor, for a while answering in person his door-bell, and accompanying his guests to the door when they retired. His friends, observing the severe labor of these calls, provided him with a colored servant by the name of "Thomas;" but Mr. Lincoln could not always wait for Thomas's movements in attending the door, nor endure his formal courtesy in bowing them out. His new position could not easily teach him, however necessary it might be, a new mode of hospitality. With him everything must be done with entire sincerity and frankness or not at all.

The following incident, given by a writer in the "Portland Press," shows the freedom with which his home was invaded by curious callers, and the kindness with which they were received. The gentleman here spoken of had been at the Chicago convention, and when the nomination was made immediately started to see the candidate at his home. The account says: "Arriving at Springfield, he put up at a public house, and loitering upon the front doorsteps had the curiosity to inquire of the landlord where Mr. Lincoln lived. While giving the necessary directions the landlord suddenly remarked, 'There is Mr. Lincoln now, coming down the sidewalk; that tall, crooked man, loosely walking this way; if you wish to see him you will have an opportunity by putting

yourself in his track.' In a few moments the
object of his curiosity reached the point which
our friend occupied, who, advancing, ventured
to accost him thus: 'Is this Mr. Lincoln?'
'That, sir, is my name.' 'My name is R.,
from Plymouth County, Massachusetts, and
learning that you have to-day been made the
public property of the United States, I have
ventured to introduce myself, with a view to a
brief acquaintance, hoping you will pardon such
a patriotic curiosity in a stranger.' Mr. Lincoln received his salutations with cordiality, told
him no apology was necessary for his introduction, and asked him to accompany him to his
residence.

"Arriving at Mr. Lincoln's residence, he was
introduced to Mrs. Lincoln and the two boys.
After some conversation concerning the Lincoln
family of the Plymouth colony and the history
of the Pilgrim Fathers, with which Mr. Lincoln
seemed familiar, Mr. R. desired the privilege
of writing a letter to be dispatched by the next
mail. Mr. Lincoln very promptly and kindly

provided him with the necessary means. As he began to write Mr. Lincoln approached, and tapping him on the shoulder, expressed the hope that he was not a spy who had come thus early to report his faults to the public. 'By no means, sir,' protested Mr. R., 'I am writing home to my wife, who, I dare say, will hardly credit the fact that I am writing in your house.' 'O, sir,' exclaimed Mr. Lincoln, 'if your wife doubts your word I will cheerfully indorse it, if you will give me permission,' and taking the pen from Mr. R. he wrote the following words, in a clear hand, upon the blank page of the letter:

"'I am happy to say that your husband is at the present time a guest in my house, and in due time I trust you will greet his safe return to the bosom of his family. A. LINCOLN.'"

These calls became so frequent that they left to Mr. Lincoln and his family but few moments of quiet or privacy. His friends again came to his relief, and procured the executive chamber, a large and beautiful room in the state-house, where he received, until his departure for Washington, all callers. Here he felt at liberty to have stated reception hours, and to impose more restraint upon his visitors; yet his simplicity and frankness were unchanged, as the following incidents will show.

Sitting in his reception room on one occasion, busily engaged with a friend, he noticed two young men timidly lingering about the door. They were dressed in rustic clothes, and gave evidence that they were unused to the presence of great men. Mr. Lincoln discerned at once that they had a desire to speak to him, but were afraid to enter. Going to the door he said kindly, "How do you do, my good fellows? What can I do for you? Will you walk in and sit down?"

Thus made to feel at their ease in his presence, the shorter one of the two made known their errand. He said he had told his companion, in a talk about the matter, that he thought him just as tall as Mr. Lincoln, and they had come to find out if he was right.   Mr. Lincoln stepped back into the room and returned with his cane. "Here, young man," he said, speaking to the taller one, "stand against the wall under this cane."   He then adjusted it to his height. "Now," he continued, "step out and let me stand under it."   He then placed himself under the cane, as the young man held it, moving his head back and forth to ascertain if it just reached it.   "There," said he, smiling, as he stepped out, "you and I are just of a height; your friend has made a remarkable guess."

He shook hands with them cordially as they parted, not giving them the slightest occasion to think that he felt his dignity offended by the nature of their call.   Soon after the young men had retired a plainly-dressed and honest-looking countrywoman entered, and introduced herself as one with whom he had been acquainted on his " circuit."   He did not at once recognize her, but she readily brought their acquaintance to his recollection by several incidents such as were sure to attend upon any period of Mr.

Lincoln's history. This point gained, she wished to remind him of a dinner of bread and milk which he once ate at her house. Mr. Lincoln could not remember *that;* he remembered taking several very excellent dinners with her, but he could not remember one upon bread and milk. "Why," said the good woman, with kindling emotions, "you called once quite late. We had been to dinner, and I felt bad because I had nothing but bread and milk to give you. You ate that, and when you had done you exclaimed, 'I have had a good dinner; *good enough for the President of the United States!*'" It was the impression that these last words made upon her mind, now revived and deepened by his prospect of being President, which caused her to walk that morning eight miles to repeat them to Mr. Lincoln, feeling perhaps that they were a prophetic assurance of his success.

Some of the calls he received conveyed much less honest expressions of friendship; while still others were of a more serious character, being from men who bore a sincere burden of mind for the future good of the republic, and who came with words of counsel and encouragement. It can be stated as a simple fact, that all these callers left Mr. Lincoln's presence with the impression that he was a remarkable man.

CHAPTER XXI.

THE WHITE HOUSE ENTERED.

ON the sixth of November, 1860, Abraham Lincoln was elected President of the United States. While the telegraph was yet flashing the exciting particulars of the voting, he retired to the privacy of his own house. His nervous system had been greatly taxed, and he threw himself upon a lounge in his chamber. Great burdens were in prospect for him, and he rejoiced with trembling. Shades of sadness, so frequent at a later period, passed across his countenance. Strange imaginings, which he could not throw off, disturbed him, and gave him, as he remarked, "a little pang, as though something uncomfortable had happened."

Mrs. Lincoln shared his gloomy forebodings, and expressed the fear " that though he might be

13

elected to a second term of office, he would not see life through the last term."

Though Mr. Lincoln had these fears in reference to himself, he had none concerning the extension and final triumph of the principles for which he had just been appointed President. The great mass of the pious people of the North had prayed for his election, and were now rendering thanks to God. Joy prevailed in the free states, anger and fierce resolutions of resistance among the slaveholders.

After his election, Mr. Lincoln's receptions at the executive chamber of the state-house became more burdensome. The log-cabin boy of the West had become the lion of the nation. Multitudes came to see him daily, to whom he spoke freely and sincerely. To a few he opened the deepest feelings of his heart.

There was an earnest Christian friend having an office adjoining the reception room, with whom, after the pressure of the public receptions, he held deeply interesting and confidential conversations. On one occasion he expressed to him the anxiety he felt to have the support of Christians, especially the aid of all ministers of the Gospel. It gave him pain to learn that any of these were opposed to the measures he was elected to support. He declared earnestly his faith in the Christian's God. Dark clouds of rebellion were gathering at the South, giving tokens of the approaching storm; but he told his friend that God was in these movements to overrule them for his glory; that he had a deep conviction that divine wrath was to be poured out upon the people, and that he was to be an actor in the struggle, though he might not live to see the end. He spoke eloquently of the solemn grandeur of the Bible descriptions of God's wrath, repeating many passages, especially from Revelation, with great power.

It was one of Mr. Lincoln's faults that these deep religious feelings were expressed only to his most intimate Christian friends. To others, immediately after the most solemn utterances, he conversed of common, and not unfrequently

of the most trifling matters.   This was largely
owing to marked peculiarities of mind, together
with a great lack of religious instruction in his
youth and early manhood.   But it was a grave
fault.   The deeper spiritual experience of later
years, with its increased light, modified, but
did not wholly remove it.

Soon after his election Mr. Lincoln visited
Chicago.   The people became wild with delight at the sight of him, and the children, as
might be expected, shared the general joy.
One little fellow, who was led by the hand into
the parlor where Mr. Lincoln was sitting, as he
caught sight of him shouted, " Hurrah for Lincoln !" at the same time taking off his hat and
swinging it over his head in true political
style.   It was a refreshing episode to the
President elect from the dull formality of hand-
shaking.   He caught the little fellow in his
strong hands, and tossing him toward the ceiling, exclaimed, " Hurrah for *you !*"

At another time, while on this visit, a little
German girl was seen by him approaching

timidly. "What do you want, my little girl? what can I do for you?" said the President. "I want your name," she replied. "But there are many other little girls that want my name, and as I cannot give it to them all, they will feel hurt if I give it to you." Assured by his pleasant and familiar manner, the little girl looked round upon her companions and replied, "Only *eight* of us, sir." Mr. Lincoln could not resist this childlike confidence, so he sat down amid the pressure of eager visitors, and taking eight sheets of paper, wrote a line or two and his name upon each, and the little girls bore away their mementoes, with blessings upon the good President.

On the 11th of February, 1861, Mr. Lincoln turned away from his home in Springfield, Ill., and from the warm and sincere friends of earlier days, and set his face toward Washington. Already the enemies of his country were making gigantic efforts to destroy the government he loved better than any other earthly good. His own life was threatened, it having been determined by banded traitors to kill him on his journey. From the platform of the railroad car which was to convey him and his family away from his neighbors he spoke these words:

"My friends, no one not in my position can appreciate the sadness I feel at this parting. To this people I owe all that I am. Here I have lived more than a quarter of a century. Here my children were born, and hēre one of them lies buried. I know not how soon I shall see you again. A duty devolves upon me which is greater, perhaps, than that which has devolved upon any other man since the days of Washington. He never could have succeeded except for the aid of Divine Providence, upon which he at all times relied. I feel that I cannot succeed without the same divine aid that sustained him, and on the same Almighty Being I place my reliance for support; and I hope you, my friends, will pray that I may receive that divine assistance without which I cannot succeed, but with which success is certain. Again I bid you all an affectionate farewell."

These farewell words were borne by the telegraph to every part of the country. The people were somewhat surprised at their decided religious character, so seldom do statesmen honor God from their high places. Some called them "cant," and deprecated their utterance; but none who knew Abraham Lincoln had reason to doubt their sincerity, though none, unfortunately, could then know how *little* these serious words expressed of the much he really *felt* of his dependence upon God.

The journey to Washington was attended by a general outburst of popular favor and confidence. Mr. Lincoln replied cordially to the many greetings which he received, and in every speech showed how deeply he felt the responsibilities which he was about to assume. The reports of these occasions thus speak of the multitudes which thronged him, and his bearing in their midst: "People plunged at his arms with frantic enthusiasm, and all the infinite variety of shakes, from the wild and irrepressible pump-handle movement to the dead grip, was exe-

cuted upon the devoted dexter and sinister of
the President.   Some glanced at his face as
they grasped his hand;   others invoked the
blessings of Heaven upon him; others affection-
ately gave him their last gasping assurance of
devotion ; others, bewildered and furious, with
hats crushed over their eyes, seized his hand in
a convulsive grasp, and passed on, as if they
had not the remotest idea who, what, or where
they were."

Of the President the reporter says: "At
first the kindness and amiability of his face
strikes you; but as he speaks the greatness
and determination of his nature are apparent.   Something in his manner, even more
than in his words, told how deeply he was
affected by the enthusiasm of the people, and
when he appealed to them for encouragement
and support, every heart responded with mute
assurance of both.   There was the simplicity
of greatness in his unassuming and confiding
manner, that won its way to instant admiration.
He looked somewhat worn with travel and the

fatigues of popularity, but warmed to the cordiality of his reception."

Mr. Lincoln was fully aware, while thus honored by the multitude, that the enemies of the holy cause of human freedom, which he so largely represented, were seeking his life. An attempt was made to throw the train from the track which bore him from Springfield. At Cincinnati hand grenades were found concealed in the cars. The government were apprised of these purposes, and a vigilant police force was put upon the track of the conspirators. A detective of great skill and experience undertook the management of the investigations. His keen search was entirely successful, and when Mr. Lincoln arrived at Philadelphia he was made acquainted with the whole plot. The persons and the exact plans of the assassins were known. Mr. Lincoln had an interview, at his hotel, with the detective, and, when he had heard his story, a way of escape was agreed upon. Mr. Lincoln had two engagements the next day, one to raise the American flag on

Independence Hall, and another to address the
Pennsylvania legislature at Harrisburgh. Both
of these engagements he declared he would
keep at the risk of his life. The plan of the
plotters, twenty in number, was to crowd about
his carriage as friends on his arrival at Baltimore, and first shoot Mr. Lincoln, and then, by
throwing hand grenades among the attendants,
and into the crowd, escape amid the slaughter
and confusion. After Mr. Lincoln's interview
with the detective, and soon after he had
retired to rest, he was aroused by the announcement of a messenger from Senator Seward and
General Scott, who had learned, independently
of the detective, of an attempt upon his life,
and who urged the necessity of an immediate
and quiet entrance into Washington. The
messenger returned on learning the plans
of the detective. On the next day, Friday, the
President met his engagements, and retired
weary, late in the afternoon, to his hotel at
Harrisburgh for rest. The people expected to
greet him again when he should enter the train

the next morning, on his return to Philadelphia. Remaining in his room until about six
o'clock, he quietly left with a military friend,
and, taking a carriage, soon entered a railroad
train in waiting for him. The telegraph wires
were cut just before the train left, that no news
of his departure might go before him. He
arrived at Philadelphia at half past ten, and
was accompanied by the detective in a carriage
to the depot of the Philadelphia and Baltimore
Railroad, where the train was about starting,
having been detained fortunately fifteen minutes beyond its appointed time. They entered
the sleeping car, passed quietly through Baltimore without changing cars, and arrived in
Washington at six o'clock Saturday morning.
A friend, sent by Mr. Seward, was anxiously
waiting with a carriage, and Mr. Lincoln was
soon surrounded by his friends at Willard's
hotel. The news of his safe arrival in Washington flew over the country with lightning
swiftness. His family were permitted to pass
unmolested to their journey's end, as the in-

tended victim had preceded them. Mr. Lincoln's enemies were vexed and astonished at his escape, and, to cover their mortification, set afloat the pure fiction of his stealing into Washington in disguise. If it had been so, they only who made the necessity would have deserved the shame.

On the fourth of March Mr. Lincoln delivered his inaugural address on a platform at the east front of the capitol, and then took the oath of office, administered by Chief Justice Taney. Bitter enemies had determined that he should not see that moment. They meant to interpose the weapons of death. But his friends rushed to the capital in large numbers, and the veteran General Scott laid his plans of defense with great skill. Most of all, God watched over his chosen instrument for the emancipation of an oppressed race, and thus that night the Forest Boy of the West entered the White House.

CHAPTER XXII.

THE NATION'S "GREAT TROUBLE."

WHEN Mr. Lincoln was a humble backwoods young man he could sit in his cabin door, and look upon the grand old oak or the wide prairie, and admire and enjoy the beauty of his situation. In the White House, built and beautified by a nation's wealth, and furnished with elegance, he was not allowed a single moment of leisure to sit down and enjoy his elevated position. The rebellion of the South began several months before he became President. All through the war which followed he spoke of it sadly as "the great trouble." On the day that he became the head of the nation seven Southern states had shot away from the bright constellation of the Union into the darkness of secession, and only about a week later they agreed to form themselves into a group called the confederacy, with its chief center at Richmond, Va.   Mr. Lincoln had told the Southern people that he was for peace; that he would not march soldiers into their territory if they did not first make war; that he wished to execute the laws made by Congress, and protect every part of the country in the enjoyment of its rights.   But the rebels would not listen to his kind words.   He was for peace, but they were for war.   Their leading men, who had held office at Washington under the President who had just left the White House, had sent many thousands of the arms belonging to the United States into the South, and the rebels stole them from the arsenals.   They took all the forts, with few exceptions, which were on their coasts.   These did not belong to them, but to the whole people.   A gallant little band in Fort Sumter, Charleston harbor, refused to surrender to them, and they immediately raised against them, on the nearest land, fortifications armed with many heavy guns, and occupied by twelve thousand fighting men.

The rebel rulers marched soldiers toward Virginia, and boasted that their flag should wave over Faneuil Hall, the cradle of American liberty. They wanted to provoke Mr. Lincoln to commence the war, that they might lay the blame of it upon him. But he had said to them at first, "We are not enemies, but friends. We must not be enemies. Though passion may have strained, it must not break our bond of affection." He continued to use the same kind language.

While the rebels in the South were thus making war upon him, Mr. Lincoln was surrounded by enemies in Washington. They were found among the office-holders, among the officers of the army and navy, in the mansions of the rich, and in the crowded hotels, as well as among the multitudes which thronged the streets. What could he do? whom could he trust? It was a dreadful time. Timid friends were afraid he would do too much, and so prevent a reconciliation, which they still hoped to see; while those who knew the rebels best were urging him to bolder measures. Through all these anxious days of suspense Mr. Lincoln was enduring exhausting labors. Office-seekers thronged the White House. Great preparations were being made in the army and navy to put down the rebellion. To all this business he gave his personal attention, and yet many of his friends blamed him because they could not *see* his efforts, and their immediate results. While the enemies of the Union were thus bold and active, and its friends irresolute and distrustful of one another, the rebels attacked and took Fort Sumter. This was on the afternoon of April 12, 1861. The guns against Sumter roused the loyal people as from a deep sleep. They could not before believe that the South were really so foolish and wicked as to mean to make war. Now they said, they have chosen war, and for no good reason; let them have war. It was plain now to the mass of the people that the Southern leaders wished a government to perpetuate and increase slavery, and if this was to be a free country, if there was to be any

free country in the world, they must be con-
quered.

Mr. Lincoln soon learned that he now had
friends. He called for seventy-five thousand
soldiers. When the rebel leaders heard of this
call they greeted it with a shout of laughter;
but when the freemen of the North heard of it
they responded with deeds rather than words.
They did not *laugh*, for they knew that war
was a serious and awful business. It was to
them the call of *duty*, and the farmer left his
untilled field, the mechanic his workshop, the
scholar his pursuit of knowledge, and even the
theological student left his sacred studies for
the camp and battle-field. The poor heard the
call and shouldered the musket, feeling that
they owed the comfort of their quiet homes to
the government which the slaveholders, always
the oppressors of the poor, meant to destroy;
the rich, and the sons of the rich, who had been
tenderly reared, shared, in the ranks, the hard-
ships of the humblest. A man from Rhode
Island, worth a million of dollars, who had just

14

purchased a passage ticket for Europe, where
he expected to travel for pleasure, tore up the
ticket and enlisted. The uprising was of God,
for none but the divine power could so have
wrought upon the hearts of a whole people.
Party feeling was for the time lost in the general desire to crush the rebellion. Party leaders, who had been zealous political enemies,
shook hands, and labored together with one
heart. Mr. Lincoln's old opponent, Mr. Douglas, called upon him, with a mutual friend, two
days after the fall of Sumter. He called to tell
Mr. Lincoln he was with him in his efforts to
save the government from the hands of traitors.
Mr. Lincoln read to him the proclamation for
seventy-five thousand men, which he had decided to send to the people the next day.
" Make it two hundred thousand," exclaimed
Mr. Douglas; " you do not know the dishonest
purposes of the rebels as well as I do." From
that time these two great statesmen worked
together. Mr. Lincoln's call for the men, and
Mr. Douglas's approval of the measure, went

forth by telegram the next morning. Mr. Douglas's voice was a trumpet call in Mr. Lincoln's favor to tens of thousands of strong men. Massachusetts was a few hours in advance of all others in the promptness with which she sent men to the President's aid. Some of her *Sixth Regiment* heard the call at midnight, and left their beds, and traveled many miles before daylight to join their companions. On its way through Baltimore, on the nineteenth of April, it was attacked by a mob carrying a secession flag, and several of its members were killed or wounded. This murderous opposition to men marching to the defense of a common capital was, at a later period of the war, nobly disowned by the legislature of Maryland. That body did what it could to wipe out the stain upon its honor made by these lawless citizens, and kindly provided for the dependent friends of those who were killed.

The sad incident at Baltimore only increased the zeal of the volunteers all over the country. " The mighty winds blew from every quarter to fan the flame of the sacred and unquenchable fire." From that time Mr. Lincoln had an army, and never again did the rebel leaders *laugh* at his power! The Hon. George Bancroft, in his " Memorial Address," thus speaks of the bearing and efforts of Mr. Lincoln and the loyal people during this " great trouble :"

" When it came home to the consciousness of the Americans that the war which they were waging was a war for the liberty of all the nations of the world, for freedom itself, they thanked God for giving them strength to endure the severity of the trial to which he put their sincerity, and nerved themselves for their duty with an inexorable will. The President was led along by the greatness of their self-sacrificing example ; and as a child in a dark night, on a rugged way, catches hold of the hand of its father for guidance and support, he clung fast to the hand of the people, and moved calmly through the gloom. While the statesmanship of Europe was mocking at the hopeless vanity of their efforts, they put forth such miracles of

energy as the history of the world had never
known.   The contributions to the popular loans
amounted in four years to twenty-seven and a
half hundred millions of dollars ; the revenue of
the country from taxation was increased seven-
fold.   The navy of the United States, drawing
into the public service the willing militia of the
seas, doubled its tonnage in eight months, and
established an actual blockade from Cape Hat-
teras to the Rio Grande ; in the course of the
war it was increased fivefold in men and in
tonnage, while the inventive genius of the
country devised more effective kinds of ord-
nance, and new forms of naval architecture in
wood and iron.   There went into the field, for
various terms of enlistment, about two million
of men, and in March last (at the close of the
war) the men in the army exceeded a million.
. . . In one single month one hundred and six-
ty-five thousand men were recruited into service.   Once, within four weeks, Ohio organized
and placed in the field forty-two regiments of
infantry, nearly thirty-six thousand men ; and

Ohio was like other states in the east and in the west. The well-mounted cavalry numbered eighty-four thousand; of horses and mules there was bought from first to last two thirds of a million. In the movement of the troops science came in aid of patriotism, so that, to choose a single instance out of many, an army twenty-three thousand strong, with its artillery, trains, baggage, and animals, was moved by rail from the Potomac to the Tennessee, twelve hundred miles, in seven days. On the long marches, wonders of military construction bridged the rivers, and wherever an army halted ample supplies awaited them at their ever-changing base. The vile thought that life is the greatest of blessings did not rise up. In six hundred and twenty-five battles and severe skirmishes blood flowed like water. It streamed over the grassy plains; it stained the rocks; the undergrowth of the forests was red with it; and the armies marched on with majestic courage from one conflict to another, knowing that they were fighting for God and liberty. The organization of

the medical department met its infinitely mul-
tiplied duties with exactness and dispatch. At
the news of a battle the best surgeons of our
cities hastened to the field to offer the untiring
aid of the greatest experience and skill. The
gentlest and most refined of women left homes
of luxury and ease to build hospital tents near
the armies, and serve as nurses to the sick and
dying. Besides the large supply of religious
teachers by the public, the congregations spared
to their brothers in the field the ablest ministers.
The Christian Commission, which expended
more than six and a quarter millions of dollars,
sent nearly five thousand clergymen, chosen out
of the best, to keep unsoiled the religious character of the men, and made gifts of clothes and
food and medicine. The organization of private
charity assumed unheard-of dimensions. The
Sanitary Commission, which had seven thousand
societies, distributed, under the direction of an
unpaid board, spontaneous contributions to the
amount of fifteen millions in supplies or money,
a million and a half in money from California

alone, and dotted the scene of war from Paducah to Port Royal, from Belle Plain, Virginia, to Brownsville, Texas, with homes and lodges."

In the darkest hours Mr. Lincoln did not despair, though he bowed before God's chastening in great sorrow. In the hours of victory he was not boastful, but gave God the glory. He hesitated long before calling upon the colored man for help; but when his duty seemed plain he put many thousands of negro soldiers into the army, and bravely did they fight for their own and the white man's freedom. He waited long for the current of events to justify the emancipation of the slaves; but when God, in these events, gave him the command, he gladly obeyed. On the first of January, 1863, he proclaimed liberty to three millions of bondmen. How the battles were fought, how victory for a long time wavered, and how, at last, it perched on the Union standards, may be learned from the histories of the war. We will turn from the strife of the battle-field to become more acquainted with him on whom the burden so heavily bore.

CHAPTER XXIII.

LOG-CABIN SIMPLICITY AT THE WHITE HOUSE.

WE have seen Abraham Lincoln among the humble laborers of the forest, a child of nature, in his intercourse with others never assuming superiority over the most lowly, nor assuming to be what he was not to obtain the favor of the great. As forest boy, farmer, surveyor, lawyer, and politician, he had never yet "put on airs" toward any he had ever known as friends. But as President, sitting in a chair more honorable than a throne, and having a power greater than that of any king or emperor, surrounded by the mighty men of his own people and the representatives of all the great nations of the world, could the common people approach him freely? could the *poor* tell him their wrongs and sorrows, and obtain his sympathy and help? could his log-cabin friends of earlier and humbler days be admitted to his presence, and be recognized on the old familiar terms? These are natural inquiries, and such as did actually interest the masses of the American people when Mr. Lincoln entered the presidential mansion. We shall answer them by such well-attested facts as have come within our knowledge.

Mr. John Hanks, a relative of Mr. Lincoln, his playmate in boyhood, and his helper in splitting rails and making log-cabins, shall be the first witness. The following testimony was received, by the writer of this volume, from Mr. Hanks's own lips. He says: "Soon after Mr. Lincoln's first inauguration I called at the White House, and sent up my name. I trembled a little, but said to myself, Don't I know Abe Lincoln, and don't he know John Hanks? Still the thought kept crowding into my mind, Abe's a long way out of sight of John now. Soon the messenger returned, saying, The President says, Come up. I entered the office where Mr. Lincoln was sitting, surrounded, it seemed to me, by all the great men of the country.

Rising from his seat, and stepping forward to meet me, he seized my extended hand with both of his, exclaiming, 'John, I'm glad to see you! How do you do? How is your family?' It was the welcome of other years, and I forgot that he was President, and replied: 'I'm pretty well, I thank you, Abe; how's your folks?' After we had chatted a while he asked me to come again, and I did call upon him several times, and he never seemed to feel above his old friend of the Illinois log-cabin."

Mr. Lincoln spoke of the reception-room in the White House as "this place," and sometimes more familiarly as "the shop," and remarked jocosely, when he was going to attend the tedious business and ceremonious calls there, that he was going to "open shop." Tuesdays and Fridays he met his counselors, the heads of the several great departments of government, in a private "cabinet meeting." All other week-days his reception-room was open. Callers were requested to wait in the ante-chamber, and send in their cards; and from the cards laid before

him he had visitors ushered in, giving prece-
dence to acquaintance. Three or four hours
each day they poured in, succeeding each other
rapidly, and nine out of ten asking for office.
He heard all patiently, and spoke to all in a
manner so natural and easy as to make them
feel entirely free in his presence.

Having given the testimony of his Illinois
friend concerning his frankness in the White
House, we will call upon Goldwin Smith, a distinguished Englishman, and a professor in one
of his country's great universities, for his impression of Mr. Lincoln at the executive mansion.
He says : " You pass into the President's room
of business through an ante-room, which has no
doubt been passed by many an applicant for
office and many an intriguer. There is no
formality, nothing in the shape of a guard ; and
if this man is really ' a tyrant worse than Robes-
pierre,' he must have great confidence in the
long-sufferance of his kind. The room is a common office, the only ornament which struck the
writer's eye being a photograph of John Bright.

"Mr. Lincoln's manner and address are perfectly simple, modest, and unaffected, and therefore free from all vulgarity in the eyes of all not vulgar themselves. The language of the President, like his demeanor, was perfectly simple. He did not let fall a single coarse or vulgar phrase, and all his words had a meaning."

Mr. Carpenter, the painter of the picture "Signing the Emancipation Proclamation," thus speaks of his first interview with Mr. Lincoln. He had formed the purpose of painting such a picture, and having obtained a letter of introduction to the President from the Hon. Mr. Lovejoy, he directed his steps toward the White House. He says: "My first interview with the President took place at the customary Saturday afternoon public reception. Never shall I forget the thrill which went through my whole being as I first caught sight of that tall, gaunt form through a distant door, bowed down, it seemed to me, even then, with the weight of the nation he carried upon his heart, as a mother

carries her suffering child, and thought of the
place he held in the affection of the people, and
the prayers ascending constantly, day after day,
in his behalf. The crowd was passing through
the rooms, and presently it was my turn and
name to be announced. Greeting me very
pleasantly, he soon afterward made an appointment to see me in the official chamber directly
after close of the 'reception.' The hour named
found me at the well-remembered door of the
apartment, that door watched daily with so
many conflicting emotions of hope and fear by
the miscellaneous throng gathered there. The
President was alone, and already deep in official
business, which was always pressing. He received me with the frank kindness and simplicity so characteristic of his nature, and after
reading Mr. Lovejoy's note, said: 'Well, Mr.
Carpenter, we will turn you in loose here and
try to give you a good chance to work out your
idea.' . . . The President seemed much interested in my work from the first, but as it
progressed his interest increased. I occupied

Viewing Carpenter at Work on the Picture.

for a studio the spacious 'state dining-room' of
the White House in the southwestern corner of
the mansion. He was in the habit of bringing
many friends in to see what advance I was
making from day to day, and I have known him
to come by himself as many as three or four
times in a single day. It seemed a pleasant
diversion to him to watch the gradual progress
of the work, and his suggestions, though sometimes quaint and homely, were almost invariably
excellent. Seldom was he ever heard to allude
to anything which might be construed into a
personality in connection with any member of
the cabinet. On one occasion, however, I remember with a sly twinkle of the eye he turned
to a senatorial friend whom he had brought in
to see the picture, and said, 'Mrs. Lincoln calls
Mr. Carpenter's group, *The Happy Family.*'
. . . There was a satisfaction to me simply in
sitting in the room with him, though no words
might be uttered, perhaps, for long intervals.
Apparently absorbed with my pencil, and he
with his papers, he would sometimes seem to

forget my presence entirely. It was at such times that I loved to study him. Frequently when persons were admitted upon business, before entering upon confidential discussions, they would turn an inquiring eye upon me, which Mr. Lincoln would meet by saying, ' O, you need not mind him; he is but a painter.' There was never a feeling of restraint or constraint on my part; his personal magnetism was so great, to hear him was like getting into the sunshine! As I now look back upon those privileged days, my heart is stirred with affection for the just and noble man, second only to the filial regard due a parent. It has been my fortune to mingle quite freely, in my professional life, with many distinguished public men. I have said repeatedly to friends, that I never knew one so utterly unconscious of distinction or power as Mr. Lincoln. He seemed to forget himself in the magnitude of his responsibilities. Under all circumstances he was precisely the same—plain, unostentatious, truth-loving, pure, and good. Dr. Stone, his family physician in

Washington, once said to me, 'I tell you, Mr. Lincoln *is the purest hearted* man I ever knew.'"

Mr. Lincoln was at one time about to leave the White House for a drive to the "Sailors' Home." The carriage was at the gate, and "the Black Horse Cavalry" in attendance as a guard. As Mr. Lincoln reached the iron fence a plain-looking man approached him timidly. He had a difficulty which he desired the President to settle for him. Mr. Lincoln stopped, threw his arm over the fence, placed his foot upon its stone foundations, and patiently heard the man while he, slowly and with great diffidence, told his complaint. When he had finished, Mr. Lincoln took a card and pencil, and, sitting down upon the low stone coping, almost seeming to sit upon the pavements, wrote upon the card to the official concerned, "Examine this man's case." People passing by looked at the head of the nation thus seated, and then at one another, seeming to say, "How undignified." The President's absorbing thought was how he could lift a burden from one of the citizens of

15

the republic, however humble.   The deed done, two hearts went lighter to their respective ways.

Mr. Lincoln's frankness is strikingly shown in his treatment at the White House of his colored guests.   His honest, hearty cordiality knew no difference of race or condition.

The first call upon the President of Frederick Douglass, the well-known antislavery lecturer, was one of mutual satisfaction.   Some months afterward Mr. Lincoln, hearing that Mr. Douglass was in the city, desired to consult him on points of executive duty, in reference to which he thought his opinion valuable.   The presidential carriage was sent to his boarding-house with the message, "Come up and take a cup of tea."   The invitation was accepted, and the President and his guest enjoyed a pleasant chat.   Mr. Douglass remarked afterward, that by no word or look during the interview was he made to feel that he was a negro.

An earnest friend of the much-wronged negro republic of Hayti was once urging upon Mr. Lincoln his desire that the United States should

" recognize " that government, and, thinking to make the matter more acceptable to him, remarked that probably the President of Hayti would send, as a representative to Washington, not a negro, but some one of the educated men of mixed blood, who might be regarded as a Spanish American white man. Mr. Lincoln replied with much animation, " I don't see the necessity for that. An educated black man would be as dignified, I have no doubt, as a ginger-colored one."

Toward the close of one of the public " receptions," in the early part of Mr. Lincoln's administration, when the rush of visitors was in a measure abated, a group of negroes in their " finest " attire were seen in earnest consultation on the lawn in front of the executive mansion. Finally they started together, and ascended the stairs to the reception room. They approached the President hesitatingly; but the moment he saw them he stepped forward to meet them, saying, " I am glad to see you," giving each a hearty shake of the hand. When they reached the street again they paused, and sent up a shout for "Linkum," which was followed by more quiet exclamations of "God bless Mr. Linkum," as they disappeared down the crowded street.

Three little girls, daughters of a mechanic, neatly but plainly dressed, went into the White House one reception day. After curiously gazing, as they were swept along in the crowd, first at the President and then at the objects about them, not having courage to offer him their . hands, as others did, they were about to pass by. But Mr. Lincoln saw them, and called out, "Little girls, are you going to pass me without shaking hands?" He then left unnoticed for a moment all others, and, stooping over, shook the hand of each child.

A lady who was visiting Washington wrote the following incidents, which came under her own observation, to her friends in Massachusetts: "A negro came to ask the President for a pass, and *remonstrated* with him because he told him he must go to get advice from a certain officer.

'But it is all the way to the Capitol,' said the
negro, ' and it is so cold to-day. I can tell you
myself that I am all right.' So the President
yielded, and heard him prove his locality by
asking questions of him. An Irish boy came
in about the same time, and Mr. Lincoln said,
'Well, did you get the place?' 'No, sir; I
want another recommend.' 'Where is the one
I gave you?' 'I lost it.' 'Careless! I have a
great mind not to give you another.' It was
the father of the nation dealing with his children; generally patient, but sometimes fretted."

It would have been remarkable indeed if Mr.
Lincoln had never "fretted," nor shown indignation at the spirit and conduct of some who
approached him for favors.

Two women once came into the reception-
room to urge some request which they deemed
very important. The younger one, not meeting
with the success she desired, used very saucy
language to the President. This was going a
little too far, and he called "Old Daniel," and
bid him show them the way out of the room.

The indignant servant obeyed with a hearty good-will.

A man who had been an officer in the army, but was dismissed in disgrace, came with his complaints to Mr. Lincoln. He heard his story, and told him he could do nothing for him. But the man would not be refused, and not only wearied him by his continual coming, but finally used insulting language. The President did not feel that he ought to suffer that without re-proof. He laid aside his papers, arose calmly, but with an earnestness before which the offend-er quailed, led him to the door, and thrust him out, saying, "Sir, I give you fair warning, never to show yourself in this room again. I can bear censure, but not insult."

Such evidences of exhausted patience very seldom occurred at the White House, but such melting scenes as the following were frequently witnessed. It is described by the Rev. Mr. Henderson, of Louisville, Kentucky: "Among a large number of persons waiting in the room to speak with Mr. Lincoln on a cer-

tain day in November, 1864, was a small, pale,
delicate-looking boy about ten years old. The
President saw him standing, looking feeble and
faint, and said, 'Come here, my boy, and tell
me what you want.' The boy advanced, placed
his hand on the arm of the President's chair,
and, with bowed head and timid accents, said :
'Mr. President, I have been a drummer in a
regiment for two years, and my colonel got
angry with me and turned me off. I was taken
sick, and have been a long time in hospital.
This is the first time I have been out, and I
came to see if you could not do something for
me.' The President looked at him kindly and
tenderly, and asked him where he lived. 'I
have no home,' answered the boy. 'Where is
your father?' 'He died in the army,' was the
reply. 'Where is your mother?' continued the
President. 'My mother is dead also. I have
no mother, no father, no brothers, no sisters,
and,' bursting into tears, he added, ' no friends ;
nobody cares for me.' Mr. Lincoln's eyes filled
with tears, and he said to him, ' Can't you sell

newspapers.?' 'No,' said the boy; 'I am too weak, and the surgeon of the hospital told me I must leave, and I have no money, and no place to go to.' The scene was wonderfully affecting. The President drew forth a card, and addressing a certain official, to whom his request was law, gave special directions to 'care for this poor boy.' The wan face of the little drummer lit up with a happy smile as he received the paper, and he went away convinced that he had one good and true friend at least in the person of the President."

One of Mr. Lincoln's old friends and his wife, from the West, visiting Washington, were recognized with the cordiality of their former interviews. On one occasion they received at their hotel, from the White House, a card inviting them to a ride in the presidential carriage. While waiting its arrival the question arose whether he should receive the President in gloves, the article never having been used by either of them in the days of their former acquaintance, except as a protection from the cold.

In the mean time Mr. Lincoln, as he was about stepping into his carriage, was discussing the same question. The ladies in both cases advised gloves, and the friend put his on, while Mr. Lincoln compromised the matter by putting his into his pocket, to be used as occasion suggested.

When the parties were well seated in the carriage, Mr. Lincoln began slyly to draw on his gloves, while the friend was as diligently working his off. Discerning the state of affairs, they both burst into a hearty laugh, which the President enjoyed exceedingly, and they were soon talking earnestly together ungloved, and on the old familiar footing.

A good-sized volume might be made of such illustrations of Mr. Lincoln's freedom from the pride of station, and his maintenance of a child-like simplicity of character while in the exercise of an official power which shaped the destinies of millions of the human race.

We shall next observe him a little more closely, and shall find that in the nobler qualities of the heart he is equally worthy our study.

CHAPTER XXIV.

TENDERNESS AND SYMPATHY.

THE dreadful consequences of the slaveholders' war, which made so many desolate homes and so many bleeding hearts, came of course immediately under the President's notice. None knew the sorrows of the people better than he, and none felt them more keenly. He did not hide himself in his immediate official duties, and keep individual suffering out of sight. He rather sought to know that he might relieve it. He brought from the log-cabin to the White House not only a cordial greeting for all classes of the people, but also a desire to promote their welfare to the full extent of his influence. Having such feelings, it is not strange that the soldiers and their friends should have been the special subjects of his kind solicitude.

In the summer of 1862 a young man belong-

ing to a Vermont regiment was tried for sleeping at his post, and sentenced to be shot. The
day was fixed for the execution, and the young
soldier prepared calmly for his fate, without
even requesting efforts for his pardon. But the
President had been informed of the sentence,
and he gave the case his immediate attention.
He learned that the youth had been brought
under sentence of death by a noble effort, not
only to do all his own duty to his country, but
also to aid a fellow-soldier in the discharge of
his. He had been on duty one night, and on
the following night he volunteered to take the
place of a companion whom he deemed too sick
to stand guard himself. On the third night he
was again called out ; but nature was too strong
for his manly resolution, and sleep overpowered
him at his post. Mr. Lincoln signed his pardon,
and sent it to the camp. The morning before
the execution having arrived, the President, not
having heard whether the pardon had reached
the officers concerned, began to feel uneasy.
He ordered a telegram to be sent to the camp,

but received no answer. State papers could not fix his thoughts, and the burdens of the nation at large could not banish from his mind the critical situation of the periled soldier-boy. He must *know* that he was safe. He ordered the carriage, and over a dusty road and beneath a scorching sun rode rapidly ten miles. Having ascertained that the pardon was received and the execution averted, he returned to busy himself again in great concerns, and to forget perhaps the incident; but the one whose life was saved did not forget it, nor fail of the deepest gratitude. Before coming to the war he had given his heart to God, and he had lived a Christian life in camp. In pardoning him the President had not only secured his continued prayers, but increased their fervency. When the campaign opened in the following spring the young man was with his regiment near Yorktown, Va. They were ordered to attack a fort, and he fell by the first volley of the enemy. His comrades caught him up, and bore him, bleeding and dying, from the field.

"Bear witness," he said, "that I have proved myself not a coward, and I am not afraid to die." Then, making a last effort, his dying breath was spent in a prayer for Abraham Lincoln!

A personal friend of the President says he called upon him in the early part of the war, and found him holding in his hand the freshly signed pardon of a young soldier who had been sentenced to be shot for sleeping at his post. He remarked, as he read it to his friend, " I could not think of going into eternity with the blood of this poor young man upon my skirts. It is not to be wondered at that a boy raised on a farm, probably in the habit of going to bed at dusk, should, when required to watch, fall asleep ; and I cannot consent to shoot him for such an act."

The body of this young man was found among the dead on the bloody field of Fredericksburgh. Near his heart lay the photograph of his preserver, under which was written, "God bless President Lincoln."

A poor washerwoman of Troy had a son, weak in mind, but strong in body. Some villainous "enlisters" persuaded him into the army, and put the bounty money into their pockets. The poor mother for a long time, in vain, sought her boy about the city. Finally, learning that he had entered the army, she found her way to Washington. Friendless, poor, not knowing what New York regiment her son was in, what could she do. She failed for some time to see the President, but finally intercepted him in his walk from the War Department to the White House. No darkened brow nor cold words repelled the suffering mother. He heard her story, took out a card, wrote the boy's name and residence, and sent it to the War Department, with the command:

"Find this poor boy, and return him to his mother.　　　　　"A. Lincoln."

"Old Daniel," the well-known servant at the White House, tells the following story to Mr. Carpenter: A poor man of Philadelphia had furnished a substitute for the army, but was

afterward made intoxicated by some wicked
companions, and thus induced to enlist. Vexed
with himself, and all concerned in the matter,
he deserted soon after reaching the army, was
arrested, tried, and sentenced to be shot. He
was to die on Saturday, and on the preceding
Monday his wife, with a babe in her arms, was
watching at the door of the President's reception-room. For nearly three days she waited
in vain. At the end of the third day the President was passing by the ante-room through a
private passage to go for rest and refreshment
to his room. Daniel says: "On his way through
he heard the baby cry. He instantly went back
to his office and rung the bell. 'Daniel,' said
he, 'is there a woman with a baby in the ante-
room?' I said there was, and, if he would
permit me to say it, I thought it was a case he
ought to see, for it was a matter of life and
death. He said, 'Send her to me at once.'
She went in, told her story, and the President
pardoned her husband. As the woman came
out from his presence her eyes were lifted, and

her lips moving in prayer, the tears streaming down her cheeks. I went up to her, and pulling her shawl, said, 'Madam, it was the baby that did it.'"

A correspondent of the Chicago Tribune relates the following anecdote: "I dropped in upon Mr. Lincoln, and found him busily engaged in counting greenbacks. 'This, sir,' said he, 'is something out of my usual line; but a President of the United States has a multiplicity of duties not specified in the Constitution nor acts of Congress; this is one of them. The money belongs to a poor negro, who is a porter in the Treasury Department, who is at present very sick with the small-pox. He is now in the hospital, and could not draw his pay, because he could not sign his name. I have been at considerable trouble to overcome the difficulty, and get it for him. I am now dividing the money, and putting by a portion labeled with my own hand, according to his wish;' and his excellency proceeded to indorse the package very carefully."

During a reception day, after a crowd of eager seekers had been in the presence of Mr. Lincoln, it came at last the turn of a woman who had been long and anxiously waiting. She was somewhat advanced in years, and plainly clad, a faded shawl being thrown over her shoulders, and a much worn hood covering her head. Her story, simply stated, was of itself an eloquent appeal. Her husband and three sons, all she had, had enlisted. Her husband had been killed in battle. Could she ask less of the country to whom she had given so much than the return of her eldest son? The President heard this request, and said, "Certainly, if her prop was taken away, she was justly entitled to one of her boys," and he immediately wrote an order for the discharge of the eldest. She gratefully took the order, and sought him at the encampment of his regiment; but the burden of her sorrowing heart was increased on learning that the object of her love and search had been wounded in a recent battle, and lay sick in a hospital. She reached the side of his

cot only in time to comfort his dying moments
with a mother's blessing. She saw him laid in
a soldier's grave, and hastened again to the
President with his order, on the back of which
was stated by the surgeon of the hospital the
sad facts concerning the one it was intended to
discharge. He was much moved by her story,
and said, "I know what you want me to do
now, and I shall do it without your asking. I
shall release to you your second son." Taking
up his pen, he began to write the order, while
the almost broken-hearted but deeply grateful
woman stood at his side, and passed her hand
fondly over his head, and stroked his rough hair
as she would have done that of her own boy.
When he had finished writing he handed her
the paper, his full heart finding relief in tears,
and said, "Now you have one of the two left,
and I have one; that is no more than right."
She took the order, and, placing her hand again
reverently upon his head, while the tears
streamed down her cheeks, and her voice fal-
tered with emotion, said, "The Lord bless you,

Mr. President. May you live a thousand years, and may you always be the head of this great nation."

Not only the petitions of suffering men and women reached the ears and touched the heart of President Lincoln, but the requests of *children* even were heard and answered. The children of Concord, Mass., sent him a "memorial," asking for the freedom of all slave children. He did not toss it aside with a sneer, saying, What do boys and girls know about such great matters? but sat down and wrote with his own hand the following beautiful letter:

"Tell those little people I am very glad their young hearts are so full of just and generous sympathy, and that, while I have not the power to grant all they ask, I trust that they will remember that God has, and that, as it seems, he *wills* to do it.   "A. Lincoln."

To the officers of the government, high in influence, and nearest to him in power, the members of his cabinet, he showed the same childlike tenderness and freedom from arrogance or jealousy. At the close of the war Mr. Stanton, the popular Secretary of War, offered Mr. Lincoln, in writing, his resignation, saying that he had accepted the office to see the rebellion ended, and now that the war was over he wished to be relieved. He added that he could bear a heartfelt tribute to Mr. Lincoln's constant friendship and faithful devotion to the country. Mr. Lincoln's generous emotions toward his secretary almost overcame him. He tore in pieces the paper containing the resignation, and, throwing his arms about Mr. Stanton's neck, exclaimed, " Stanton, I cannot spare you ! You have been a good friend and faithful public servant. It is not for you to say when you will no longer be needed here." The friends of both were present, and were melted to tears by the incident.

On the Monday before his death, being on his way from Richmond to Washington, Mr. Lincoln stopped at City Point, on the James

River. He called upon the head surgeon there, and told him he wished to visit every hospital under his charge, and shake hands with every soldier. The surgeon expressed his surprise, and remarked that he was not probably aware how severe his task would be, for there were in the hospitals at least six thousand men. Mr. Lincoln smiled, and replied that he "guessed he was equal to the task; at any rate he would try, and go as far as he could. He should never probably see the boys again, and he wanted them to know that he appreciated what they had done for their country."

As the surgeon was not able to turn Mr. Lincoln aside from his purpose, they commenced their rounds together. The President went to the bedside of each, shaking hands with all, speaking words of cheer to some, making kind inquiries of others, and receiving from all the heartiest welcome. In one of the wards lay a wounded rebel soldier, receiving the same care as the rest; he watched the tall form of Mr. Lincoln with deep interest as he passed from one to the other, and, as he approached his bedside, he raised himself on his elbow in bed and extended his hand, exclaiming in tears, "Mr. Lincoln, I have long wanted to see you to ask your forgiveness for raising my hand against the old flag." Mr. Lincoln wept freely, and taking the hand of the penitent rebel, he assured him of his forgiveness and good-will.

When the tour of the hospitals was made, Mr. Lincoln returned to the surgeon's office. He had scarcely entered when a messenger came, saying one ward had been omitted, and "the boys" wanted to see their President. Though tired, back he went, and finished his proposed task.

When they had again entered the office, the surgeon expressed the fear that Mr. Lincoln's arm would be lame with so much hand-shaking. "I guess not," said the President; "I have strong muscles," and stepping immediately to the door, he took up a heavy ax and began to chop a large log of wood. The chips flew in every direction under his vigorous strokes, showing something of the "muscle" of his log-cabin days. Pausing, he held the ax out steadily at full arm's length. Strong men who stood by, men accustomed to hard labor, vainly tried to do the same thing. The President then returned to the office and took a glass of lemonade, refusing anything stronger, while the chips "which Father Abraham chopped" were being gathered up as mementoes.

Such was the sympathy and tenderness of the *people's* ruler, "a true born king of men."

CHAPTER XXV.

PLEASANT HUMORS.

THE "jokes" of Mr. Lincoln have been repeated wherever his name has been spoken,
and they have become known much better than
the feelings of the heart from which they
flowed. They appear to many as the evidence
of a trifling mind, and as utterances made
when silence or seriousness would have been
wiser. Those who judge thus have not learned
what wisdom was often conveyed in his simple,
well-told "story;" what sharp rebuke to an
impertinent teaser; what gentle refusal to a
solicitation to which his kindness could not
interpose a direct "no;" and especially, what
relief to his overburdened, almost crushed
heart. Those who have read only Mr. Lin-
colns "jokes," and read perhaps as his many
silly and coarse remarks which he never

uttered, do not know that his habitual and life-
long feeling was one of sadness. "His was the
saddest countenance I ever knew," said the
artist who studied it for six months. Mr. Bancroft eloquently says: "Mr. Lincoln was a man
of infinite jest on his lips, with saddest earnestness at his heart." Said his little son, in the
agony of his grief on learning that his father
was shot, and being assured by a friend that he
had gone to heaven, "Then I am glad he has
gone there, for he was *never* happy here."

A gentleman who was his law partner for
twenty years thus sketches this feature of his
character: "Mr. Lincoln was a sad-looking
man; his melancholy dripped from him as
he walked. His apparent gloom impressed his
friends, and created a sympathy for him, one
means of his great success. He was gloomy,
abstracted, and joyous, rather humorous, by
turns. I do not think he knew what real joy
was for more than twenty-three years."

Mr. Lincoln's *pleasant humors* were the natural relief of his burdened spirit. The follow-

ing touching incident contains Mr. Lincoln's own statement of this fact. On one of the darkest days of 1862, when a heavy gloom hung over the country, and when the news of fresh disaster had just been announced, a deeply earnest loyal member of Congress called upon the President, who, after the first salutation, commenced telling a humorous incident. The congressman was in no mood to hear, and, starting up, said, "Mr. President, I did not come here this morning to hear stories; it is too serious a time." Instantly the smile upon Mr. Lincoln's face gave way to an expression of the deepest seriousness. "Sit down again, sir," he said, in a tone of tender earnestness; "I respect you as an earnest, sincere man. You cannot be more anxious than I am constantly, and I say to you now that were it not for this occasional *vent* I should die!"

The sending forth of a proclamation to emancipate millions of slaves was a great responsibility, and Mr. Lincoln felt it to be such. He watched the course of God's providence, he

thought deeply and prayed fervently in relation
to the subject. When he at last decided to
issue it, and had written it out carefully, he
called his cabinet together to read it to them.
What a solemn moment! Mr. Lincoln saw
clearly the vast consequences of that document,
and felt keenly his relation to them. What he
saw and felt was weighing down his mind too
heavily for the reading and conversation which
the occasion required. He must have some
relief. Before naming the business of the
meeting, he took down from a shelf a volume,
" Artemus Ward—His Book," read a whole
chapter of its drollery, and laughed most heartily. Few could understand the propriety of
this, perhaps there was no propriety in it, and
fewer could desire or enjoy such reading at
such a time. But to Mr. Lincoln it was like a
draught of fresh air to a man gasping for breath.
He laid down the book refreshed, and the expression of his countenance, the tone of his
voice, and his whole manner instantly changed.
If his dignified audience were before disgusted,

they were now awed, as he announced the
object of the meeting, and read the document
which was to make tyranny tremble, and to
rejoice the hearts of the friends of freedom
throughout the world.

Mr. Lincoln kept some work of wit and
humor in a corner of his desk, so that, when
exhausted with labor or over-pressed with care,
he could take it out, and give fresh elasticity to
his mind by the perusal of a few pages. Once
when he had been sorely beset continually from
seven in the evening until nearly twelve, and
while still surrounded by men high in office,
and by numerous large documents demanding
attention, he pushed all aside, and assuming an
easy and comical air, said to one of the party,
" Have you seen the Nasby Papers? There is
a chap out in Ohio who has been writing a
series of letters in the newspapers over the sig-
nature of Petroleum V. Nasby. Some one sent
me a collection of them the other day. I am
going to write to Petroleum to come down
here, and I intend to tell him if he will com-

municate his talent to me I will *swap* places with him." Mr. Lincoln, on finishing these remarks, took a copy of the letters from his desk, read one to the company, laughed heartily, and obtained from it the brief relief that many statesmen would have sought from a glass of brandy or wine. He then tossed the book aside, and returned to his exhausting labor, his countenance at once assuming its melancholy earnestness.

We have seen, in the course of our sketch of Mr. Lincoln, how pungent he often made his " little story " in argument, and how powerful in drawing the masses to him. A few illustrations of these facts are at hand. Mr. Lincoln had met the rebel " Peace Commissioners " on board a steamer near Fortress Monroe. After a brief discussion, the conversation turned to the slavery question. Mr. Stephens, the chief speaker for the commissioners, said : " If the South should consent to peace on the basis of the Emancipation Proclamation the Southern society would be ruined; no work would be

done because the slaves would work only upon
compulsion, nothing would be cultivated, and
both blacks and whites would *starve*. This was
raising a dust in which no peace negotiations
could be made, so Mr. Lincoln *settled* that line
of argument by the following story: "Mr.
Stephens," he said, addressing the rebel vice-
president with a roguish twinkle of his eye,
"*you* ought to know a great deal better about
this matter than *I*, for you have always lived
under the slave system. I can only say in reply
to your statement of the case, that it reminds
me of a man out in Illinois by the name of Case,
who undertook, a few years ago, to raise a very
large herd of hogs. It was a great trouble to
feed them, and how to get around this was a
puzzle to him. At length he hit upon the plan
of planting an immense field of potatoes, and
when they were sufficiently grown he turned
the whole herd into the field, and let them have
full swing, thus not only saving the trouble of
feeding the hogs, but also that of digging the
potatoes! Charmed with his sagacity, he

stood one day leaning against the fence counting his hogs, when a neighbor came along. 'Well, well, Mr. Case,' said he, this is all very fine. Your hogs are doing very well just now, but you know that out here in Illinois the frost comes early, and the ground freezes a foot deep. Then what are they going to do?" This was a view of the case Mr. Case had not taken into the account. Butchering time for hogs was way on in December or January. He scratched his head, and at length stammered, 'It may come pretty hard on their *snouts*, but I don't see but that it will be, *Root, hog, or die.*'"

The conversation of the commissioners was turned immediately to other features of the grave question in hand.

Mr. Lincoln's stories were used by him to good purpose in shutting off mistaken efforts on the part of his friends to lessen his charity toward his political opponents. He disliked any conversation which had this tendency, and was very apt, when it began, to be *reminded* of something laughable which put the gossiper off

his track.   A friend on one occasion was rising
seven times in reference to the course of opposition to Mr. Lincoln taken by two prominent
members of his party, when he interrupted him
by saying: "It's not worth fretting about; it
reminds me of an old acquaintance, who, having
a son of a scientific turn, bought him a micro-
scope. The boy went around experimenting
with his glass upon everything that came in his
way. One day at the dinner table his father
took up a piece of cheese. 'Don't eat that,
father,' said the boy, 'it is full of *wrigglers!*'
'My son,' replied the old gentleman, taking at
the same time a huge bite, 'let 'em *wriggle;* I
can stand it if they can.'"   .

Mr. Lincoln's ever-ready story was wonderfully potent in turning aside any unpleasant
differences between his associates in the government, or those high in office about him. When
General Grant came into chief command of the
armies, Mr. Stanton, the Secretary of War, at
their first interview could not agree with him
as to the number of troops to be left for the

defense of Washington while the main army
marched on Richmond.   A correspondent of
the "New York Herald" thus gives the conversation, and the happy turn given to the dispute
between these high officials :

"Well, General," remarked the Secretary, " I
suppose you have left enough men to strongly
garrison the forts around Washington ? "

"No," said Grant coolly ; "I couldn't do that."

"Why not ? " cried Stanton nervously, "why
not ? why not ? "

" Because I have already sent the men to the
front," replied Grant calmly.

"That wont do," cried Stanton, more nervous than before.   " It's contrary to my plans.
I can't allow it.   I'll order the men back."

" I shall need the men there, and you can't
order them back," answered Grant.

"Why not ? " inquired Stanton again. "Why
not? why not ? "

" I believe that I rank the Secretary in this
matter," was the quiet reply.

"Very well," said Stanton, a little warmly,

"we'll see the President about that. I'll have to take you to the President."

"That's right," politely observed Grant. "The President ranks us both."

Arrived at the White House, the General and the Secretary asked to see the President upon important business, and in a few moments the good-natured face of Mr. Lincoln appeared.

"Well, gentlemen," said the President, with a genial smile, "what do you want of me?"

"General," said Stanton stiffly, "state your case."

"I have no case to state," replied General Grant. "I am satisfied as it is;" thus outflanking the Secretary, and displaying the same strategy in diplomacy as in war.

"Well, well," said the President, laughing, "state your case, Secretary."

Secretary Stanton obeyed; General Grant said nothing; the President listened very attentively. When Stanton had concluded, the President crossed his legs, rested his elbow on his knee, twinkled his eyes quaintly, and said:

"Now, Secretary, you know we have been trying to manage this army for two years and a
half, and you know we haven't done much with
it. We sent over the mountains and brought
Mister Grant, as Mrs. Grant calls him, to manage it for us, and now I guess we had better let
Mister Grant have his own way."

Nobody *ranked* the President, so this was decisive; but no doubt the feelings of the Secretary were saved by the manner and spirit in
which he was overruled.

Mr. Lincoln not only used his pleasantries to
take the offense from a refusal, but at other
times to give a zest to a favor granted. A German paper publishes the following illustration
in point: " A lieutenant, whom debts compelled
to leave his fatherland and the service of his
country, succeeded in being admitted to President Lincoln, and, by reason of his commend-
able and winning deportment, together with his
intelligent appearance, was promised a lieutenant's commission in a cavalry regiment. He
was so enraptured with his success that he

deemed it his duty to inform the President that he belonged to one of the oldest families of the nobility of Germany. 'O, never mind that,' said Mr. Lincoln, ' you will not find that to be an obstacle in the way of your promotion.' "

We cannot further detail these pleasant humors, which show more plainly than any mere description could do, the sincere and noble nature of Abraham Lincoln. The following is a pleasing testimony to their moral character by Mr. Carpenter, the artist, and familiar friend of the President: "I feel that it is due to Mr. Lincoln's memory to state, that during the entire period of my stay in Washington, after witnessing his intercourse with almost all classes of people, including governors, senators, members of Congress, officers of the army, and familiar friends, I cannot recollect to have heard him relate a circumstance to any one of them all, that would have been out of place uttered in a ladies' drawing-room. . . . What I have stated is a voluntary testimony from a standpoint, I submit, entitled to respectful consideration."

CHAPTER XXVI.

CONFIDENCE IN GOD.

OUR acquaintance with Mr. Lincoln thus far has shown us that from his childhood he reverenced the name of God. Though associated with men who used profane language, he never formed the wicked habit of swearing. From his mother's lips he had heard the truths of the Bible, and early learned to love the study of its sacred pages. As soon as he was elected President the nation began to hear from him serious reference to his sense of dependence upon God for strength and wisdom in his great work. When he entered upon the duties of the presidential office, his messages and proclamations expressed more confidence in God, and breathed more of the spirit of true piety, than had ever before been manifest in the head of our republic. The earnest Christians of the country were of course es-

pecially pleased with this; but they knew that he
might do and say all this and yet not love Christ.
They desired to be assured that he was not
merely *almost* a Christian, but a truly converted
man; they wanted him *to be* and *to profess* himself such, that the light of his example might
shine forth from his high station, and thus glo-
rify his Father in heaven.

It was with this feeling that some Christians
in a western state said to a gentleman who was
going to the White House on important business,
"We want you to ask Mr. Lincoln *if he loves
Jesus.*" The gentleman visited Washington,
had an interview with the President, and after
his business was finished said : "At the solicitation of some Christian friends, I have a question
to propose to you if you will allow me, Mr. Lincoln." "Certainly," was the courteous reply.
"*Do you love Jesus?*" inquired the gentleman.
The President burst into tears, buried his face
in his handkerchief, and for a time was unable
to speak. He at length said : "When I left
Springfield I said to my fellow-citizens, 'Pray

for me ;' but I was not then a Christian. When
my child died, soon after I entered upon my
office, my heart was still rebellious against God.
I was not then a Christian. But when I walked
the battle-field of Gettysburg, and saw the
wounded and the dying, and felt that by that
victory our cause was saved, I then and there
resolved, and gave my heart to Jesus. *I do love
Jesus.*"

A lady of our acquaintance, with whom we
conversed just before sitting down to write this
page, says: "I was frequently brought into Mr.
Lincoln's presence in reference to the soldiers of
the hospitals for whom I was laboring, and I
once asked him why he was not a member of
some Church, as I believed he was a real
Christian. He evaded the question, giving me
a general answer, and intimated his great un-
worthiness for such a solemn and responsible
relation." The lady adds: "I always found
Mr. Lincoln ready, and even pleased to converse
upon the subject of experimental religion, but
he was extremely modest respecting his own

experience." As Mr. Lincoln was able to say sincerely that "he loved Jesus," .it was a sad mistake, from whatever cause he was led into it, that he did not become a member of the Church and a receiver of the sacraments, thus confessing Christ before men, according to his commandment. If he had done so he might have been restrained, by the known sentiments of the Church, from attendance upon the theater, where occasion was given for his violent death.

But it is pleasanter to leave this subject to the Christian charity of those who have candidly studied Mr. Lincoln's religious character, and pass on to other evidences of his confidence in God and the Bible.

During one of the darkest days of the rebellion, a delegation of Christian men called upon the President. "We trust the Lord is on our side," said the gentleman who spoke in their behalf. "I do not consider that as essential as something else," replied the President. The pious visitors looked surprised, until he added:

"I am most concerned to know that we are on the Lord's side."

The following illustrates Mr. Lincoln's love of the Bible, and his habit of reading it while he was President. It is related by the Rev. Mr. Adams, a Presbyterian clergyman of Philadelphia. He was on a visit to Washington, and had made an appointment to call upon the President at the White House at five o'clock in the morning. Says Mr. Adams: "Morning came, and I hastened my toilet, and found myself at a quarter to five in the waiting room of the President. I asked the usher if I could see Mr. Lincoln. He said I could not. 'But I have an engagement to meet him this morning.' 'At what hour?' 'At five o'clock.' 'Well, sir, he will see you at five.' I then walked to and fro for a few moments, and hearing a voice, as if in grave conversation, I asked the servant, 'Who is talking in the next room?' 'It is the President, sir.' 'Is anybody with him?' 'No, sir, he is reading the Bible.' 'Is that his habit so early in the morning?' 'Yes, sir; he spends

every morning from four to five in reading the
Scriptures and praying.' "

The central act of Mr. Lincoln's administration, and, as he himself has said, "the great
event of the nineteenth century," was the sending forth of the proclamation to emancipate the
slaves. In the performance of this great duty
he had constantly prayed that it might be in
accordance with God's will. Just before it was
done, a delegation of clergymen from Chicago
called upon him to urge the speedy performance
of the act. The President said to them: "I can
assure you the subject is on my mind day and
night, more than any other ; *and whatever shall
appear to be God's will I will do.*"

At the cabinet meeting on the Saturday before the proclamation was issued, Mr. Lincoln
said in a low tone, after giving other reasons
for it, "and I have promised God that I would
do it." Secretary Chase, who was sitting near
him, wishing to be sure that he understood him
aright, said, "Did I understand you, Mr. President ?" Mr. Lincoln replied, "I made a sol-

emn vow before God, that if General Lee was driven back from Pennsylvania I would crown the result by the declaration of freedom to the slave."

Once, when greatly perplexed by the difficulties which surrounded him, he exclaimed hopefully to a distinguished senator, " The Lord has not deserted me thus far, and he is not going to now."

A pious lady, who acted as a nurse to one of Mr. Lincoln's sick children, relates several incidents illustrating his religious feelings. At the news at one time of a sad defeat of the Union forces he was very much depressed, but said : " I have done the best I could. I have asked God to guide me, and now I must leave the event with him."

On another occasion, when a great battle was in progress at a distant and important point, he manifested great solicitude. The lady remarked, " You can trust, and you can at least pray." " Yes," said he, in a tone which expressed the relief he felt in the suggestion, and taking up his Bible, started for his room. There, with God's word opened before him, he pleaded on his knees its gracious promises of support. So earnest were his supplications in his secret chamber that his voice was heard by those in the sick room of his family. While he yet prayed, God sent him the answer of peace. At one o'clock a telegram announced a Union victory. On receiving it, he came directly into the sick room, his face beaming with joy, exclaiming: "Good news! good news! The victory is ours, and God is good!"

"Nothing like prayer," suggested the pious lady.

"Yes there is," replied Mr. Lincoln, "praise. Prayer and praise!"

A colored woman by the name of Johnson, of rare ability, earnest piety, and very many good works in the hospitals of the soldiers, in her ardent love for the President prepared as a present for him a magnificent collection of wax fruit. It was set upon a "stem-table" highly ornamented, and she proceeded, in company with her minister, to Washington, to present it in person. She says: " The commissioner, Mr. Newton, received us kindly, and sent the box to the White House, with directions that it should not be opened until I came. The next day was reception day, but the President sent me word that he would receive me at one o'clock. I went and arranged the table, placing it in the center of the room. There I was introduced to the President and his wife. He stood next to me, then Mrs. Lincoln, Mr. Newton, and the minister. Mr. Hamilton, the minister, made an appropriate speech, and at the conclusion said: ' Perhaps Mrs. Johnson would like to say a few words.' I looked down to the floor and felt that I had not a word to say; but after a moment or two the fire began to burn, and it burned and burned until it went all over me. I believe it was the Spirit; and I looked up to him and said: 'Mr. President, I believe God has hewn you out of a rock for this great and mighty purpose. Many have been led away by bribes of gold, of silver, of presents; but you have stood firm because God was with you, and if you are faithful to the end God will be with you.' With his eyes filled with tears Mr. Lincoln walked round and examined the present, pronounced it beautiful, thanked me kindly, and said: '*You must not give me the praise; it all belongs to God.*'"

A few months before the close of Mr. Lincoln's earthly labors, two hundred members of the Christian Commission waited upon him at the White House. Mr. Stuart, chairman of the Commission, addressed a few words to him, referring to the debt which the country owed him. "My friends," replied Mr. Lincoln, "you owe me no debt of gratitude for what I have done, and I," raising his arm and swinging it through the air, expressive of a desire to be understood, "and I, I may say, owe you no gratitude for what you have done; just as, in a sense, we owe no gratitude to the men who have fought our battles for us. I trust that this has all been for us a work of duty." At the utterance of this word *duty*, Mr. Lincoln's sad face shone with a divine radiance, his whole soul seeming on fire with a spiritual baptism, while in eloquent language he gave God all the glory for the light which had dawned upon the Union cause, and for the prospect of a speedy and complete triumph.

Mr. Stuart, catching fully the spirit of the occasion, said, "Mr. President, with your permission, we will have, *here* and *now*, a word of prayer." Mr. Lincoln assented with an ease and cordiality which showed that the suggestion fully accorded with his own feelings; and Bishop Janes there, in the east room, led in a brief and fervent petition.

Such are a few of the many incidents in Abraham Lincoln's public career, which show his habitual love for the Bible and his confidence in God.

CHAPTER XXVII.

THE WHITE HOUSE HOME.

THE White House during Mr. Lincoln's presidency was, as we have seen, not a place barred to the outward world by embarrassing ceremonies, and repelling dignity of position. The family circle was reached by the known rules and simple courtesies of common life. We shall guard against breaking over these with obtrusive rudeness, while we seek a familiar acquaintance with Mr. Lincoln in his easy movements of intercourse with his family and confidential friends. It is here often that the springs are seen which give direction and force to public character, and here that a photograph may be taken of a man *as he is*, and not as he appears when dressed for the public observation.

It was much easier for a person of Mr. Lin-

coln's previous habits and natural frankness, to
give the curious world a too ready access to his
privacy, than to make any part of the White
House at any time a genuine family home; so it
happens that his inner home life there is well
understood.   But even here he is most highly
esteemed when best known.

Mr. Lincoln was an early riser.   The hour
between four and five was devoted to the reading of the Bible and prayer, which furnished
divine wisdom and strength for the duties of
the day.   The next two hours were generally
devoted to an examination of the mail, with the
aid of his private secretary, often giving his
personal attention to letters from even the
humblest sources.   A visit to the War Office, or
to his nearest chief military commander, frequently came in before, followed, or interrupted
his morning examination of the mails.   A
glance at the newspapers, too, was obtained
during these two hours.

Thus five hours were given to devotion and
public business before breakfast, which was

18

eaten at nine. This was succeeded by weary hours of pressing business. At four he declined seeing company, and often took a carriage drive with some member of his family. The dinner at six was frequently one of generous hospitality to personal friends, and the evening hours following were devoted to easy, informal, social intercourse.

The above indicates only a very *general* disposition of the President's time, for his kindness of heart allowed numerous interruptions, so numerous, indeed, as to become sometimes more the rule than the exception. We have seen that his sleeping-room even was invaded at the midnight hour by friends imploring mercy for the condemned, and that the moments devoted to rest and refreshment were relinquished at the cry of a babe and the petition of its sorrowing mother.

A member of Congress, and personal friend of Mr. Lincoln, thus speaks of him as he appeared in the family circle: "His intercourse with his family was beautiful as that with his

friends. I think that father never loved his
children more fondly than he. The President
never seemed grander in my sight than when,
stealing upon him in the evening, I would find
him with a book open before him (as you have
seen him in the popular photograph) and little
"Tad" beside him. There were, of course, a
great many very curious books sent to him, and
it seemed to be one of the special delights of
his life to open those books at such an hour
that this boy could stand beside him, and they
could talk as he turned over the pages, the
father thus giving to the little fellow a portion
of that care and attention of which he was or-
dinarily deprived by the duties of office pressing
upon him.

This son Thomas, or "Tad," was an especial
favorite with his father. He welcomed him to
his presence, though engaged by pressing business or with distinguished personages. The
presidential steamboat excursions down the
Potomac were generally accompanied by Tad.
At one time, while going to Fortress Monroe,

the petted boy naturally abused his privilege of unrestrained access to his father, much to his annoyance, and the annoyance of the invited friends of the excursion. "Tad," said the President, whose conversation with the party he interrupted, "if you will be a good boy, and not disturb me any more till we get to Fortress Monroe, I will give you a dollar." The bribe served as a restraint for a while, but long before the boat reached the fort Tad was as noisy as ever; but just before landing he confidently approached the President, saying, "Father, I want my dollar." His father turned, and, looking a tender reproof, said, "Tad, do you think you have earned it?" "Yes," replied Tad boldly. Mr. Lincoln paused for a moment, and cast at the lad a half reproachful glance; then, taking out his pocket-book, he handed him a dollar bill, saying, "Well, Tad, at any rate I will keep *my* part of the bargain."

Tad at one time went over to the War Office, and the Secretary of War, indulging in the same humor toward the White House pet as the father, commissioned him "lieutenant." Tad, however, made a serious matter of his authority, and ordered a quantity of muskets to be sent to the house. At night he discharged the guards who were on duty at the executive mansion, and, ordering up the gardeners and servants, put guns into their hands, drilled them, and put them on duty in place of the guard. His elder brother, Captain Robert Lincoln, learning of Tad's audacity, reported the proceedings to his father, requesting that they might be stopped. Mr. Lincoln, however, treated the affair as a good joke, and refused to interfere. Fortunately for the weary laborers, so unexpectedly made soldiers, the little officer in command of them presently went to bed, and they were quietly discharged. So the White House went unguarded that night, though surrounded by bitter and reckless enemies.

In February, 1862, Willie, Mr. Lincoln's son next older than Tad, died at the White House.

He is described as a remarkable boy, serious, mature above his years in intellect, and of an affectionate disposition. His sickness and death occurred at a time when Mr. Lincoln's public burdens were almost crushing. Tad was sick at the same time, and a pious lady from one of the hospitals was called in as nurse. Mr. Lincoln watched with her at the bedside of the children, and often walked the room, saying sadly, "This is the hardest trial of my life. Why is it? why is it?"

On the morning of Willie's funeral the lady said to him, "There are many Christians praying for you this morning, Mr. Lincoln." He wiped away the tears from his eyes, and replied, "I am glad to hear that. I want them to pray for me. I need their prayers." As he was going out to the burial she again uttered words of sympathy. He thanked her in a tender manner, and replied, "I will try to go to God with my sorrows." A few days afterward she asked him if he could trust God. He answered, "I think I can, and I will try. I wish I had the childlike faith you speak of, and I trust he will give it to me."

In this moment of bitter sorrow he remembered his mother, whose death had caused his first great grief, and spoke of her with deep emotion. "I remember her prayers," he said, "and they have always followed me. They have clung to me all my life."

After the funeral of little Willie, which was on Thursday, Mr. Lincoln entered upon his public duties bowed down with grief, and seeming to be lost in its all-absorbing influence. The following Thursday it completely overpowered him, and he shut himself from all society. For several weeks the recurrence of Thursday was the occasion for throwing off all business, and indulgence in unrestrained grief. His case became alarming, and his friends sought every possible means of diverting his thoughts, and turning the current of his affections. At this time Dr. Vinton, of Trinity Church, New York, happened to be visiting Washington. Some mutual friends invited him to the White House, and he was received in the parlor kindly by Mr. Lincoln. The doctor, having entered into conversation with him, tenderly chided him for so rebellious a spirit against the wise appointment of God. "Why," he added, "your son, Mr. Lincoln, is *alive* in paradise." Mr. Lincoln had listened as one whose mind was occupied with other thoughts until the words caught his ear, "your son is alive." Starting to his feet he exclaimed, "Alive! *alive!* Surely you mock me!" "No, sir; believe me," replied Dr. Vinton; "it is a most comforting doctrine, founded upon the words of Christ himself."

Mr. Lincoln looked for a moment inquiringly at the doctor, and then, stepping forward, threw his arms about his neck, and pillowing his head, with childlike simplicity, upon his breast, sobbed, "Alive! alive!"

"My dear sir," replied Dr. Vinton, twining his arm around the weeping father, "believe this, for it is God's most precious truth."

At Mr. Lincoln's request Dr. Vinton sent

him a copy of a sermon containing a more full statement of the truth which had so much comforted him.   From this time the controlling power of the President's grief was broken, and the Thursday weeping was discontinued.

CHAPTER XXVIII.

THE RAINBOW OF PEACE.

WE cannot follow the history of Mr. Lincoln, nor understand fully his character, unless we glance, at least, at the great events in the country with which he stood so intimately connected.

In the early summer of 1864, in the midst of the war, while immense armies were in the field, and a great navy was afloat, the question, Who shall be President after March 4, 1865 ? began to occupy a prominent place in the minds of the people. A convention met in Baltimore June 8, and said, It shall be Abraham Lincoln; and when the people voted in November, 1864, more than two millions of the *voters* declared it should be Abraham Lincoln, giving him two hundred and twelve of the two hundred and thirty-three votes in the electoral college. The

soldiers sent forth under the President to the
field of danger and death, said by an almost
unanimous vote, Give us again for president our
good friend, Abraham Lincoln. A German
soldier expressed the feelings of his companions
in arms when he declared, in broken English,
"I goes for Fader Abraham; he likes the soldier boy. Ven he serves tree years he gives
him four hundred dollar, and re-enlists him von
veteran. Now, Fader Abraham, he serve four
years. We re-enlist him for four years more,
and make von veteran of him."

Mr. Lincoln must, of course, have been gratified by his re-election. Not that he craved
power and honor, but the election was his loyal
countrymen's approval of his course. Mr. Carpenter, the painter, to whose recollections of Mr.
Lincoln we have several times referred, says:
"I watched him closely during the political
excitement previous to the Baltimore Convention, to see if I could discover signs of personal
ambition, and I am free to say that, apart from
the welfare of the country, there was no evi-

dence to show to my mind that he ever thought of himself."

When elected, he did not show a spirit of triumph. He said: "It is no pleasure to me to triumph over any one; but I give thanks to the Almighty for this evidence of the people's resolution to stand by free government and the rights of humanity."

His inaugural address on the 4th of March, 1865, one of the last public acts of his life, closes with the following precious words; words which will be admired more and more as they are repeated on the successive pages of history, and their true Christian spirit becomes more and more the spirit of the nations of the earth :

" With malice toward none, with charity for all, with firmness in the right, as God gives us to see the right, let us strive on to finish the work we are in, to bind up the nation's wounds, to care for him who hath borne the battle, and for his widow and orphans, to do all which may achieve and

cherish just and lasting peace among ourselves
and with all nations."

While the people were thus looking after
the continuance of right men in office, the
noble armies of freedom were gaining vic-
tories on every side over the armies of
slavery. The brave men under Butler and
Farragut at New Orleans, and under Grant
and Porter at Vicksburg, and Banks at Port
Hudson, had opened the Mississippi to the Gulf,
free forever, and cut the Confederacy in twain.
Sherman had marched South to Atlanta, and
then swept across the country eastward until
his army snuffed the breezes of the Atlantic,
and caused the hasty abandonment of Savan-
nah; and then, after a brief pause, marched
northward toward Richmond, causing the proud
and long-defiant cities of Charleston and Columbia, with all the strongholds of rebellion
in the Carolinas, to yield to the "stars and
stripes."

While Sherman thus triumphed, General
Grant was breaking down the stubborn de-

fenses of Richmond, and hemming on every
side the army of General Lee.

On the 22d of March Mr. Lincoln reached
City Point, on the James River. The rainbow
of peace was faintly spanning the heavens, and
he came to witness for himself the going down
of the last dark cloud of the rebellion. Until
Monday, April 3, he remained in his tent at
City Point. As battle after battle was gained
on well-fought and bloody fields, he tele-
graphed the results to the country. The strain
upon his nervous system was, of course, very
great. The crisis had come at last; the end of
the long conflict seemed near, but the known
uncertainty of war could not be banished from
his mind. The Union soldiers were fighting
with a sublime bravery, and being resisted with
a stubborn ferocity. Would victory pause now?
were there other lessons of humiliating defeat,
and of patient waiting, necessary to prepare
the nation for complete and final success?
From the burden of such conflicting feelings
Mr. Lincoln needed some relief, and he sought

it in a way suited to his circumstances and peculiar temperament.

There was a pet cat in his tent having a new-born family. During the painful pauses between the battles, he diverted his mind by playing with them. On Monday morning, April 3, news came that the rebels had left Richmond, and that our forces were occupying the city. He started at the instant to go up the river, but turning round as he was about to leave the tent, he took up one of the kittens, saying, "Little kitten, I must perform a last act of kindness for you before I go. I must open your eyes." Having passed his finger gently over the closed lids until the eyes were uncovered, he then put the kitten upon the floor, enjoying for a moment its surprise at the new world into which it had been introduced, and remarked pensively: "O that I could open the eyes of my blinded fellow-countrymen as easily as I have those of that little creature!"

The Fifth Massachusetts Cavalry, a colored

regiment, were the first pushed forward to learn
certainly that the enemy had fled from Richmond.   They dashed at full speed along the
road from the north side of the James River,
where they had been watching for this opportunity, and entered the almost deserted streets
of the city.   The foe was sullenly retiring from
the southern side at the same moment, the
buildings were on fire in many places, and
the fearful havoc of war was everywhere
apparent.

On the afternoon of the same day, April 3,
Mr. Lincoln reached the city.   On foot, with
no guard except a few sailors, who had rowed
him the last mile on the river, he landed from
the boat and passed through several streets of
the city.   "Tad," accompanying, held timidly
his father's hand as he gazed upon the strange
sights.   There were but few whites left in the
city, and from them Mr. Lincoln could expect
only a formal welcome.   But the blacks were
unbounded in their joy at his coming.   They
waved their handkerchiefs, tossed up their hats,

and rent the air with shouts as hearty and sincere as were ever uttered. "Glory to God! Glory! Glory! Glory!" were heard, mingled with the uproar of patriotic expressions. A colored woman, standing in her doorway, exclaimed, as she saw the passing form of him who had doubtless been blessed with her humble prayers, "I thank you, dear Jesus, that I behold President Linkum!" Another expressed her wild delight by jumping up and clapping her hands, exclaiming, "Bless de Lord! Bless de Lord! Bless de Lord!"

An aged negro pressed toward the President, and lifting his hat, while the tears rolled down his face, said, with a heart swelling with emotion, "May de good Lord bless you, President Linkum!" The President removed his own hat respectfully, and bowed his acknowledgement of the salutation.

After a brief observation of the city, Mr. Lincoln went back to City Point. On the following Thursday he returned, accompanied by Mrs. Lincoln. He then soon hastened away to

19

Washington. While he was absent, Mr. Seward, the Secretary of State, had been seriously injured by an accident, and was now confined to his bed. Mr. Lincoln went directly to his house, and, after words of kind sympathy, he threw himself across the bed, and rehearsed the story of Grant's wonderful generalship, the bravery of the soldiers, their success, Richmond's fall, and the vigorous pursuit of Lee which was then going on. The President's face glowed with animated joy during this recital, and as he closed he started up, exclaiming with intense emotion, "Now for a day of National Thanksgiving?"

Grant pursued Lee's flying and broken army with relentless vigor. On Monday, April 10, the telegram announced to the country his surrender. The cup of the nation's joy seemed full. The noise of bells and cannon, and the wild shouts of the multitude, feebly expressed the emotions of the people. There were thanksgivings in devout hearts too deep for utterance, and praise which no words could express. God had triumphed gloriously, and his name was exalted in the land. There came, too, from grateful hearts the exclamations, "Abraham Lincoln," "Our beloved Lincoln," "Our noble President." The rainbow of peace was spanning the heavens of our Republic.

CHAPTER XXIX.

THE DARK CLOUD OF SORROW.

THE morning on which it was announced that
Lee had surrendered, a crowd gathered in front
of the White House.   They had brought three
bands of music; but they wished to hear the
music of the President's voice.   He appeared at
the window above the main entrance, and was
greeted with enthusiastic shouts. "He was in
his happiest mood, but declined making a formal
speech.   He told them that he supposed arrangements were being made for a general demonstration of joy to take place in a day or two,
and that he should be expected to speak then,
and added: "I shall have nothing to say if I
dribble it out before.   I propose now closing up
by requesting you to play a certain air or tune.
I have always thought 'Dixie' one of the best
tunes I ever heard.   I have heard that our

adversaries over the way have attempted to appropriate it as a national air. I insisted yesterday that we had fairly captured it. I presented the question to the Attorney General, and he gave his opinion that it is our lawful prize. I ask the band to give us a good tune upon it."

Mr. Lincoln remained at the window while "Dixie" was being played, and then proposed three cheers for Lieutenant-General Grant and all our brave soldiers; these being given, he called for three more for "our gallant navy;" he then bowed and retired.

This was Monday, April 10, and in this cheerful frame of mind he answered all calls of duty and friendship until Friday, the 14th. To God he expressed, in public and private, the most devout gratitude, giving him the honor and glory of the victory. To his friends he uttered words of heartfelt congratulations. Toward the enemies of his country, now defeated and in his power, he breathed the spirit of forgiveness and conciliation; and even intimated, in a public speech, a generous plan, already conceived, to restore them to legal and friendly relations with the government.

Mrs. Lincoln, writing to Mr. Carpenter some months after her husband's death, thus speaks of his feelings during these days of national rejoicing, which proved to be the last of his own life: "How I wish you could have been with my dear husband the last three weeks of his life. Having a realizing sense that the unnatural rebellion was near its close, and being the most of the time away from Washington, where he had passed through such conflicts of mind during the last four years, feeling so encouraged he freely gave vent to his cheerfulness. Down the Potomac he was almost boyish in his mirth, and reminded me of his original nature as I remembered him in our own home, free from care, surrounded by those he loved. That *terrible Friday* I never saw him so supremely cheerful. His manner was even playful. At three o'clock he drove out with me in the open carriage. In starting I asked him if any one should accompany us. He immediately replied:

'No, I prefer to ride by ourselves to-day.'
During the drive he was so gay that I said to
him laughingly, 'Dear husband, you almost
startle me by your great cheerfulness!' He replied, 'And well I may feel so, Mary, for I
consider this day the war has come to a close;'
and then added, 'We must be more cheerful in
the future. Between the war and the loss of
our darling Willie we have been very miserable.'
Every word he then uttered is deeply engraved
on my poor broken heart."

On Friday morning Mr. Lincoln sent to Ford's
theater to engage a private box for the evening,
to hear the play of "Our American Cousin."
General Grant had arrived in Washington the
previous evening, and the theater managers announced in the papers the expected attendance
of the General and the President. General
Grant did not wish to attend, and so left the
city; but Mr. Lincoln's mind, as his wife states
in the letter from which we have quoted, "was
fixed upon having some relaxation," though
when the hour came he was disinclined to this

kind of entertainment. He had, at long intervals, visited the theater to relieve an overburdened brain. Since his conversion on the battle-field of Gettysburg, light concerning the sinfulness of theatrical amusements had come to
him but slowly, as it did to Christians fifty years
ago in reference to drinking ardent spirits; so,
with tearful regrets, we must follow our beloved
President to his dying chamber, through the
theater. We feel sure that if he had lived under surrounding influences of less constraining
power, or lived to greater maturity of religious
experience, he would have sought relaxation in
some way *clearly consistent with his love for
Jesus.*

The presidential carriage, containing, besides
Mr. and Mrs. Lincoln, their friends, Major
Rathbone and Miss Harris, arrived at the theater about nine o'clock. When the party entered
the box the President was greeted by the audience with prolonged cheers. He bowed his
acknowledgements, and was soon quietly observing the transactions upon the stage.

While Mr. Lincoln was thus engaged, John Wilkes Booth, a stage-player, and the son of a stage-player, entered the theater. He gradually pushed his way through the crowd in the gallery in the rear of the dress-circle to the door of a narrow passage. Deceiving the servant who stood at the entrance, by showing a card and saying that the President had sent for him, he walked in, closed and barred the door. From this passage two doors opened into Mr. Lincoln's box. Stepping lightly to the further door, which stood ajar, he shut and fastened it. He then went back and took a hasty glance through a hole which had been previously bored for the purpose in the first door, and learned the position of the persons within. Mr. Lincoln was nearest the assassin and only about four feet from him, sitting so as to expose to his view the back and left side of his head. Booth thrust his arm into the entrance, leveled his pistol, and fired. The ball entered the brain of the President, who, dropping his head on his breast, and falling slightly forward, remained perfectly still.

Booth rushed into the midst of the amazed company and shouted "Freedom." Major Rathbone, in attempting to seize him, received a deep wound upon the arm from a dagger. The assassin then dashed over the front of the box, down twelve feet upon the stage. As he fell his spurs became entangled in the folds of an American flag, and brought him suddenly to the floor with a fractured leg. Springing to his feet, he flourished his dagger, and in a theatrical tone uttered the insulting cry, "*Sic semper tyrannis,*" adding, "The South is avenged." In the confusion he fled across the stage and through the windings in the rear of the theater, mounted a fleet horse in waiting, and hastened away. He forgot that if he "should take the wings of the morning and dwell in the uttermost parts of the sea," and if he should say "Surely the darkness shall cover me," that there was One to whom "the night shineth as the day," whose hand should lead him, and whose right hand should *hold him.* In a few days he was pursued by the officers of justice, and, in his attempt to resist them, shot dead!

Mr. Lincoln was tenderly carried to a house opposite the theater, but he had no consciousness, uttered no word, and felt no pain. He gradually sunk into the arms of death, and expired the next morning at twenty-two minutes past seven. He was surrounded by the great men of the nation, who bowed in grief and wept like children. Mrs. Lincoln lay in an adjoining room, supported in her agony by her oldest son and other friends.

While these dreadful scenes were passing at the theater, a ruffian by the name of Lewis Payne Powell, in league with Booth and others, forced his way into the sick chamber of Mr. Seward, the Secretary of State, mounted his bed and stabbed him three times with a dagger. He would no doubt have killed him, but a soldier by the name of Robinson, who was acting as nurse to Mr. Seward, seized the murderer around the body while his intended victim rolled himself off the bed. Powell rushed down

stairs and out of the house, having in entering
and returning stabbed five persons, and knocked
down and stunned with the butt of a pistol
one of Mr. Seward's sons. Powell was afterward arrested, tried and hanged, as were three
others who aided in the plot, one of them a
woman.

Mr. Seward finally recovered, but for a long
time lay in a critical situation. His physician
had kept from him all knowledge of what had
happened at the theater. A few days after, he
had his bed wheeled round so that he could see
the tops of the trees in the park opposite. His
eye instantly caught the stars and stripes at
half mast on the War Department. He gazed
in silence and sadness for a moment, and then,
turning to an attendant, said, "The President
is dead!" The attendant was confused and
silent, while the Secretary added: "If he had
been alive he would have been the first to call
on me; but he has not been here, nor has he
sent to know how I am, and there's the flag at
half mast." He then gazed again in silence at

the flag, while the tears flowed freely down his gashed cheeks.

The body of the President was carried, a few hours after his death, to a room in the White House, where it was embalmed. On Tuesday the doors were opened to the public, and it is believed twenty-five thousand persons went in to view the face so familiar to them once, and now so pale in death. The rich and the poor came, the white and the black, dropping their tears together upon his coffin. Hundreds, as they pressed past, casting a hasty glance at the face so often lighted up with expressions of compassion for the oppressed, uttered a word or a sentence of deep-felt affection.

Wednesday was the day of the funeral. There was first service in the east room of the executive mansion, and then the remains were removed to the rotunda of the Capitol. It was followed by a long procession, and witnessed by a vast multitude of people. Numerous martial bands sent forth their tender strains of music. The minute guns of the adjacent forts joined in deep-toned unison. The country's flag, at half mast, drooped in pensive sadness.

At the same hour of the service at the rotunda, the churches all over the loyal states were opened for religious worship. The drapery of mourning was everywhere displayed, and sorrow was depicted on every face.

CHAPTER XXX.

THE BURIAL — BENEDICTIONS — FAREWELL.

AFTER the funeral service at Washington, the remains of the President were borne toward their western resting-place. Accompanied by the dust of his "darling Willie," they started on their long journey on the 21st of April. When the train arrived at Baltimore, where, four years before, the living President barely escaped the hand of violence, a great multitude were moved to affectionate demonstrations of grief at the sight of his bier and cold clay. At Harrisburgh the remains were exposed to view in the state capitol, and for many hours were surrounded by the weeping people.

When the approach of the funeral train to Philadelphia was announced, the whole city was moved at its coming. A new hearse had been prepared to receive the body, drawn by eight

black horses in silver-mounted harness. It was
carried to Independence Hall, where it lay from
Saturday evening until Monday morning. During nearly every hour of this time it was visited
by the people. Individuals falling into the
human current, which constantly poured through
the hall, were borne slowly along for four or five
hours before their eyes rested upon the pale face
of him for whom they grieved. They left behind them tears and flowers, the tokens of their
pity and love.

When the remains reached the city of New
York, its mighty din of business was at once
hushed. The tolling of bells and minute guns
faintly expressed the sorrow of its people. Immense throngs were in the streets to testify in
person their interest in the mournful occasion.
Thousands patiently endured the pressure of the
long, densely packed line, which moved slowly,
hour after hour, toward the City Hall, where the
corpse lay in state. The high in office, name,
and influence, united with the humble poor in
following its departure from the city, and fifteen

thousand citizen soldiers escorted the solemn procession.

At Albany and Buffalo, and through the long railroad route between those cities, *the people's* mourning was repeated. A reporter who followed the train wrote: "A funeral in each house in Central New York would hardly have added solemnity to the day." As the honored dead passed on every city had its tribute of sorrow. At Chicago the mourning began to be still more like the mourning of a household over its fallen head. The whole state of Illinois had in days past yielded to the political moulding of Mr. Lincoln's wonderful influence, and now its heart throbbed with the universal sorrow.

When the remains had arrived at Springfield, and were deposited in the State-house, they seemed to have returned to a part of his own family from which he had been long separated. Many of his early and endeared friends there had not seen him since he requested their prayers, and waved them an affectionate adieu from

20

the platform of the cars which bore him toward the White House.

The nation's honored dead reached its final resting-place May 4. It is a beautiful spot at Oak Ridge Cemetery, about two miles from Springfield. The dust of "Little Willie," who was so much loved in life, and inconsolably mourned in death, was laid beside his father's. A prayer was offered, a hymn sung, a portion of the Scriptures read, an eloquent eulogy delivered by Bishop Simpson, the benediction pronounced, and the multitude melted slowly away, leaving the dead in solemn quiet.

While thus the whole nation was bowed with grief, none mourned more sincerely than those whom Mr. Lincoln had delivered from slavery. "We have lost *our* President," was the universal feeling. The following statements and incident, given by a correspondent of the New York Tribune, writing from Charleston, South Carolina, illustrates this fact: "I never saw such sad faces nor heard such heavy heart-beat-

ings as here in Charleston the day the dreadful
news came. The colored people, the native
loyalists, were like children bereaved of an only
and beloved parent. I saw one old woman
going up the street, wringing her hands, and
saying aloud as she walked, looking straight
before her, so absorbed in her grief that she
noticed no one:

"'O Lord! O Lord! O Lord! Massa Sam's
dead! Massa Sam's dead! O Lord! Massa
Sam's dead!'

"'Who's Massa Sam?' I asked.

"'Uncle Sam,' she said; 'O Lord! O Lord!'

"I was not quite sure she meant the President, and said again:

"'Who's Massa Sam, Aunty?'

"'Mr. Linkum,' she answered, and resumed
wringing her hands, and moaning in utter
hopelessness and sorrow. The poor creature
was too ignorant to comprehend the difference
between the very unreal Uncle Sam and the
actual President; but her heart told that he
whom heaven had sent in answer to her prayers

was lying in a bloody grave, and she and her race were left—*fatherless.*"

The news of Mr. Lincoln's death carried sorrow wherever it was published.

A distinguished minister of Montreal says in a memorial sermon: "On Wednesday last a funeral took place in Washington which closed the law courts, banks, and places of business in this chief city of British America; invested our streets with subdued silence; called out visible tokens of mourning; and opened halls and churches, where words of sorrow and sympathy might find utterance. All this was spontaneous. It was the spontaneous tribute of respect to the memory of the late President of the United States."

When the news of the assassination reached England, the excitement, the indignation and sorrow, were intense. A prominent paper declared that the people in the streets of London would have treated Booth as roughly, had he been in their power, as any in New York or Washington. The London "Times" and

" Punch," which had wounded Mr. Lincoln when wounds were the most keenly painful, hastened to lay a wreath upon his coffin. Public demonstrations of sorrow were attended by immense multitudes. The Parliament signed an address of condolence, and presented it to the American minister. The Queen wrote a letter to Mrs. Lincoln with her own hand, in which her sorrow and sympathy were expressed.

The startling tidings were received in Paris with universal and deep grief. The emperor sent an officer of his household to the American minister with assurance of his sympathy. Protestant religious bodies, popular assemblies, and literary associations, passed earnest resolutions in reference to the sad event. Two thousand young men of the Latin quarter of Paris attempted to go in a body to the United States legation, to utter, through a chosen spokesman, words of tenderness for the noble dead; but they were hindered by the jealous police, and only a few reached it to deliver the message.

A few hours after the sad news was published in Paris, its Sunday-schools were holding a general meeting in a capacious circus building having seats for four thousand persons, all of which were filled. The chairman rose and said: " My children, I had prepared a little speech for you, but a horrible fact has just been related to me. The President of the United States is dead. Abraham Lincoln has been assassinated!" He then sat down, too full of emotion to say more. Several of the ladies burst into tears. An American gentleman whispered to one of them, and inquired if she was an American lady. She replied, " No, I am French; but I have followed Mr. Lincoln's course from the beginning of the war, and feel as if his death were a personal affliction."

As the telegrams announced throughout Europe the dreadful deed, governments and people paused, and uttered words of amazement and lamentation. A recent traveler says that even Palestine, and more distant parts of

Asia, heard the name of Lincoln, and lamented his fall. The islands of the ocean, too, caught the flying sorrow. At the Sandwich Islands memorial sermons were preached, and churches were draped. The mourning of America became the mourning of the world. And this was right, for Abraham Lincoln lived and died to promote the freedom of universal humanity.

The story of our beloved Lincoln carries with it its own instructive lesson, and enforces it too. From the log-cabin to the White House, it is a story of truthfulness, temperance, love, unselfish labor, and large-hearted benevolence. Abraham the boy learned from his mother's lips to fear God and reverence the Bible, and he never departed from her instruction.

Abraham Lincoln, the man, never tired of labor, reading, and thought. But he read but little and thought much. Mr. Herndon, for twenty years his law partner, says, "He read less and thought more than any man of his standing in America, if not in the world."

Abraham Lincoln, the politician, despised trickery. At the threshold of high position, honor, and power, he was willing to lose all rather than give a bribe to those who claimed to keep the door. When challenged he paused, and indignantly exclaimed: "I authorize no bargains, and will be bound by none."

As President he exercised more than a monarch's power with wisdom and purity. When he unconsciously approached the time of his instant death, he had an increasing assurance that *he loved Jesus.*

Cordially we unite with the eloquent Bishop Simpson, and say:

"Chieftain, farewell! The nation mourns thee. Mothers shall teach thy name to their lisping children. The youth of our land shall emulate thy virtues. Statesmen shall study thy record, and learn lessons of wisdom. Mute though thy lips be, yet they still speak. Hushed is thy voice, but its echoes of liberty are ringing through the world, and the sons of bondage listen with joy. Prisoned thou art in death, and yet thou art marching abroad, and chains and manacles are bursting at thy touch. Thou didst fall not for thyself. The assassin had no hate for thee. Our hearts were aimed at, our national life was sought. We crown thee as our martyr, and humanity enthrones thee as her triumphant son. *Hero, Martyr, Friend, farewell!*"

THE END.

BOOKS FOR SUNDAY SCHOOLS.

200 Mulberry-street, New York.

MISSIONS IN WESTERN AFRICA.
Including Mr. Freeman's Visit to Ashantee. Four Illustrations. 18mo.

AN ESSAY ON SECRET PRAYER,
As the the Duty and Privilege of Christians. By JOSEPH ENTWISLE, Minister of the Gospel. 18mo.

JUVENILE TEMPERANCE MANUAL,
And Facts for the People. By D. GOHEEN, Columbia, Pa. 18mo.

SCRIPTURE PROPHECY.
Fulfillment of Scripture Prophecy, as Exhibited in Ancient History and Modern Travels. By STEPHEN B. WICKENS. Three Illustrations. 18mo.

LIFE OF THE APOSTLE JOHN.
By Rev. DANIEL SMITH. 18mo.

HISTORY OF THE PATRIARCH JACOB.
By Rev. DANIEL SMITH. Five Illustrations. 18mo.

THE LIFE OF HEZEKIAH.
By Rev. DANIEL SMITH. 18mo.

THE LIFE OF JOSHUA.
By Rev. DANIEL SMITH. Three Illustrations. 18mo.

DEAF AND DUMB.
Recollections of the Deaf and Dumb. 18mo.

THE LIFE OF ELIJAH.
By Rev. DANIEL SMITH. Five Illustrations. 18mo.

THE WATERLOO SOLDIER.
Three Illustrations. 18mo.

SUPERSTITIONS OF BENGAL:
Anecdotes of the Superstitions of Bengal, for Young Persons. By ROBERT NEWSTEAD, Author of "Ideas for Infants." 18mo.

BOOKS FOR YOUNG PEOPLE.

200 Mulberry-street, New York.

THE POET PREACHER:

A Brief Memorial of Charles Wesley, the eminent Preacher and Poet. By CHARLES ADAMS. Five Illustrations. Wide 16mo.

WORDS THAT SHOOK THE WORLD;

Or, Martin Luther his own Biographer. Being Pictures of th Great Reformer, sketched mainly from his own Sayings. B CHARLES ADAMS. Twenty-two Illustrations. Wide 16mo

MINISTERING CHILDREN:

A Story showing how even a Child may be as a Ministering Angel of Love to the Poor and Sorrowful. Wide 16mo
Illustrated

This is one of the most moving narrations in the whole list of our publications. Its sale in England has reached 40,000 copies. The illustrated edition contains more than a dozen superb cuts on plate paper.

THE MINISTRY OF LIFE.

By MARIA LOUISA CHARLESWORTH, Author of "Ministering Children," etc., etc. Five Illustrations. Wide 16mo.

ITINERANT SIDE;

Or, Pictures of Life in the Itinerancy. Illustrated. Wide 16mo.

THE OBJECT OF LIFE:

A Narrative illustrating the Insufficiency of the World, and the Sufficiency of Christ. Four Illustration. Wide 16mo.

LADY HUNTINGDON PORTRAYED;

Including Brief Sketches of some of her Friends and Co-laborers. By the Author of "The Missionary Teacher," "Sketches of Mission Life," etc. Five Illustrations.

THE MOTHER'S MISSION.

Sketches from Real Life. By the Author of "The Object of Life." Five Illustrations. Wide 16mo.

MY SISTER MARGARET.

A Temperance Story. By Mrs. C. M. EDWARDS. Four Illustrations. Wide 16mo

14

BOOKS FOR SUNDAY SCHOOLS.

200 Mulberry-street, New York.

LIFE OF ADAM CLARKE.

An Account of the Religious and Literary Life of Rev. Adam Clarke, LL.D. 18mo.

LIFE OF MRS. COKE.

Memoir of Mrs. Penelope Goulding Coke, by her Husband, the late Rev. Dr. Coke. 18mo.

LIFE OF JOSEPH COWLEY.

Sketch of the Life and Character of the late Mr. Joseph Cowley, Superintendent of Red Hill Sunday School, and Senior Secretary of the Sunday School Union, Sheffield. By John Holland, Author of the Life of Summerfield. 18mo.

A VOYAGE TO CEYLON:

With Notices of the Wesleyan Mission on that Island. By a Surgeon. 18mo.

THE CEYLONESE CONVERTS:

Brief Memoirs of Frederic Hesler and Donna Wilmina, with Interesting Notices of others in the Ceylon Schools. By Robert Newstead. 18mo.

WANDERINGS AND ADVENTURES.

Steedman's Wanderings and Adventures in the Interior of Southern Africa. Abridged by Rev. Daniel Smith. 18mo.

THE SUNDAY-SCHOOL ORATOR:

Being a Collection of Pieces, original and selected, both in Prose and Verse, for Sabbath-School Anniversaries By George Coles. 18mo.

THE LIFE OF ELISHA.

By Rev. Daniel Smith. Two Illustrations. 18mo

LIFE OF SOLOMON, KING OF ISRAEL:

By Rev. Daniel Smith. Four Illustrations. 18mo.

THE HISTORY OF SARAH BREWER,

A Poor Orphan. Four Illustrations. 18mo.

THE SOLDIER'S FUNERAL.

Illustrated. 18mo.

BOOKS FOR SUNDAY SCHOOLS.

200 Mulberry-street, New York.

THE EARLY DEAD:

Containing Brief Memoirs of Sunday-School Children. Three volumes, 18mo.

HOSTETLER;

Or, The Mennonite Boy converted. A true Narrative. By a Methodist Preacher. Two Illustrations. 18mo.

MOUNTAINS OF THE BIBLE.

Conversations on the Mountains of the Bible, and the Scenes and Circumstances connected with them in Holy Writ. Supplementary to the "Mountains of the Pentateuch." By E. M. B Four Illustrations. 18mo.

A MISSIONARY NARRATIVE

Of the Triumphs of Grace, as seen in the Conversion of Kaffirs, Hottentots, Fingoes, and other natives of South Africa. By SAMUEL YOUNG, twelve years a Missionary in that Country. 18mo.

JULIANA OAKLEY.

A Tale. By MRS. SHERWOOD, Author of "Little Henry and his Bearer." Two Illustrations. 18mo.

ERMINA:

The Second Part of Juliana Oakley. By MRS. SHERWOOD. Five Illustrations. 18mo.

THE DAIRYMAN'S DAUGHTER:

An Authentic Narrative. By Rev. LEGH RICHMOND. A new edition, comprising much additional matter. 18mo.

LITTLE JANE;

Or, The Young Cottager; The Negro Servant; and other Authentic Narratives. By Rev. LEGH RICHMOND. With Illustrations. 18mo.

LIFE OF REV. LEGH RICHMOND,

Author of the "Dairyman's Daughter," "Young Cottager," etc. By STEPHEN B. WICKENS. 18mo.

SCENES IN THE WILDERNESS:

An Authentic Narrative of the Labors and Sufferings of the Moravian Missionaries among the North American Indians By Rev. WILLIAM M. WILLETT. 18mo.

BOOKS FOR SUNDAY SCHOOLS.

200 Mulberry-street New York.

THE YOUNG MINER:

A Memoir of John Lean, Jun., of Camborne, in the County of Cornwall. By JOHN BUSTARD. 18mo.

THANET SUNDAY-SCHOOL TEACHER.

Mildred, the Thanet S. School Teacher. By JOHN BUSTARD. 18mo.

OLD HUMPHREY'S OBSERVATIONS.

Selections from Old Humphrey's Observations and Addresses. Six Illustrations. 18mo.

INTERESTING STORIES

For the Entertainment and Instruction of Young Readers. Illustrated. Two volumes, 18mo.

ELLEN AND SOPHIA;

Or, The Broken Hyacinth. By MRS. SHERWOOD, Author of "Little Henry and his Bearer." Three Illustrations. 18mo.

FARMER GOODALL AND HIS FRIEND.

By the Author of "The Last Day of the Week." With Illustrations. 18mo.

JANE AND HER TEACHER.

A Simple Story. 18mo.

THE MOUNTAIN AND VALLEY.

Two Illustrations. 18mo.

PROCRASTINATION;

Or, Maria Louisa Winslow. By MRS. H. M. PICKARD. 18mo.

CHRISTIAN PEACE;

Or, The Third Fruit of the Spirit. Illustrated by Scenes from Real Life. 18mo.

THE CAVES OF THE EARTH:

Their Natural History, Features, and Incidents. 18mo.

THE BLIND MAN'S SON;

Or, The Poor Student successfully struggling to overcome Adversity and Misfortune. Two Illustrations. 18mo.

3

BOOKS FOR SUNDAY SCHOOLS.

200 Mulberry-street, New York.

LIFE OF REV. RICHARD WATSON,
Author of Theological Institutes, Dictionary, Exposition of the Gospels, etc. By STEPHEN B. WICKENS. 18mo.

SERIOUS ADVICE
From a Father to his Children. Recommended to Parents, Guardians, Governors of Seminaries, and to Teachers of Sunday Schools. By CHARLES ATMORE. 18mo.

A VOICE FROM THE SABBATH SCHOOL:
A brief Memoir of Emily Andrews. By Rev. DANIEL SMITH. 18mo.

LITTLE JAMES;
Or, The Story of a Good Boy's Life and Death. John Reinhard Hedinguer; or, the Faithful Chaplain: being an Account of an extraordinarily Pious and Devoted Minister of Christ. 18mo.

MEMOIR OF ELIZABETH JONES,
A Little Indian Girl, who lived at the River-Credit Mission, Upper Canada. Three Illustrations. 18mo.

JERUSALEM AND THE TEMPLE.
Rebuilding of Jerusalem and the Temple; or, The Lives of Ezra and Nehemiah. By Rev. DANIEL SMITH. 18mo.

THE TRAVELER;
Or, A Description of Various Wonders in Nature and Art. Illustrated. 18mo.

MEMOIRS OF JOHN FREDERIC OBERLIN,
Pastor of Waldbach, in the Ban De La Roche. 18mo.

THE LIFE OF GEORGE WASHINGTON,
First President of the United States. By S. G. ARNOLD, Author of "Memoirs of Hannah More." Three Illustrations. 18mo.

THE LIFE OF DANIEL.
By Rev. DANIEL SMITH. Two Illustrations. 18mo.

THE LIFE OF MOSES.
By Rev. DANIEL SMITH. Illustrated. 18mo.

www.ingramcontent.com/pod-product-compliance
Lightning Source LLC
Chambersburg PA
CBHW060518030726
47498CB00004B/991